SUTTON'S SURRENDER

THE SINFUL SUTTONS BOOK 3

SCARLETT SCOTT

Sutton's Surrender

The Sinful Suttons Book 3

Published by Happily Ever After Books, LLC

Edited by Grace Bradley

Cover Design by Wicked Smart Designs

For more information, contact author Scarlett Scott.

www.scarlettscottauthor.com

For my readers, with so much more gratitude than I can properly convey.

CHAPTER 1

LONDON, 1816

Garrick Weir, Viscount Lindsey, heir to the Duke of Dryden, had ventured to the East End with his outrage, an unwise proliferation of coin, and the determination to pay off the scheming, fortune-hunting harlot who was attempting to ensnare his madcap younger brother into matrimony. Thus far, he had managed to avoid pickpockets and other would-be criminals. He had similarly surpassed guards and slipped, unscathed, to the private room where his quarry would be found. The palms he had greased on his way here had suggested she would be within shortly.

Tallying ledgers.

Apparently, the lowborn miscreant was intelligent enough to know her arithmetic, at least—if his study of the neatly penned sums before him was to be trusted—in the case of gin being purchased versus consumed by patrons. But then, one could only suppose she also possessed enough intellect to bamboozle his idiotic sibling.

To be fair, Aidan was a stripling who thought with his cock and little else. It was entirely likely all that was required to persuade him was a set of breasts and a willing cunny.

Garrick shuddered as he thought of his brother's appalling lack of judgment and turned a page in the ledger. Aidan had made it more than clear he did not give a farthing about preserving the Weir family name. Never mind that the Duke of Dryden was one of the oldest, most revered titles in England. Being a part of such a distinguished lineage was not sufficient for Aidan, who amused himself besmirching their good name by drinking, whoring, gambling, gadding about at bare-knuckle boxing matches, and announcing his intention to marry a lowborn title seeker.

His pronouncement at dinner the evening before had been the ultimate slap to the face for their father. The duke suffered from a weak heart, and Garrick had feared their father would expire at the table. Garrick did not fault their father for his outrage. Miss Penelope Sutton was the most unsuitable match Aidan could have found, save from a Covent Garden doxy. Mother had called for her hartshorn and retired to her apartments.

Garrick sifted a few more pages of the ledger, his *ennui* leading him to grudgingly admit Miss Sutton's penmanship was tidy and concise. He appreciated neatness, even from this particularly unwanted source. Her spelling was regular. Perhaps she had received *some* manner of education. Not that such a matter should concern him. After this evening, he would neither see the woman nor hear from her ever again.

A sound in the hall beyond interrupted his perusal. He straightened, moving away from the desk and assuming his most intimidating pose as the door opened. She was earlier than he had expected, but it was just as well. The sooner they could settle this disagreeable matter, the better. He had a ball to attend.

The woman standing before Garrick took him by surprise. He had imagined she would be dressed in an unseemly display, breasts nearly popping from her bodice, her gown dampened to render it sheer. But instead, she wore a modest affair of an indeterminate light hue, buttoned to the throat. Her auburn hair was bound in a simple knot, a few tendrils free to frame her face.

"Who are you?" she demanded.

Well, her rudeness certainly met—*and surpassed*—his expectations.

He bowed as if they were in a drawing room rather than a ramshackle East End gaming hell where countless despicable acts of gambling, drinking to excess, and Lord knew what else had occurred. "I am Lord Lindsey, Miss Sutton."

She remained where she was, pinning him with a narrow, hazel-eyed stare. "Am I meant to know you?"

He tamped down a surge of irritation. *Everyone* knew him.

But then, she was a little no one, wasn't she?

"You are acquainted with my brother, Lord Aidan Weir," he elaborated grimly, for he refused to acknowledge the supposed betrothal between herself and his sibling.

The marriage was never happening, and he had lowered himself to visit this intolerable haven of iniquity to make certain of that.

A frown marred her otherwise fine features. "You are Aidan's brother?"

Garrick grudgingly noted Miss Penelope Sutton was quite beautiful. Scarcely any wonder his scapegrace of a brother had been following her about these last few months, sniffing at her skirts.

"I am *Lord* Aidan's brother, as I said," he repeated, emphasizing his brother's title.

The familiarity of his sibling's name on her lips was irksome, and not just for the obvious reason.

"*Lord* Aidan." She was unsmiling, her gaze studying him from head to toe in rude fashion as she remained where she was. "Yes, of course. Forgive me for forgetting he has a brother. He does not often speak of his family."

Was that meant to be a barb? And why had the witch yet to curtsy and show the deference which was due him?

"I do not suppose he would," Garrick commented mildly. "Do you intend to hover on the threshold all evening, or will you enter, Miss Sutton?"

He was growing weary of this game. An evening of entertainment beckoned, and he did not like the manner in which his body was reacting to this brazen chit. He was far too aware of her, his entire being acutely on edge.

Anger, he told himself. That was all it was.

She is an East End fortune hunter greedy to snatch a titled gentleman as her marital prize.

But she was a lovely one, and he could not deny it, much as that fact aggrieved him.

"Why have you come?" she asked instead of answering the question he had posed, still motionless.

He sighed. "Miss Sutton, enter the room, if you please. I hardly wish for all the world to hear my private affairs. Whilst my brother does not have a care for discretion, I do, and that is why I have sought you out this evening."

"Has something happened to him?" She stepped over the threshold at last, the door not entirely closing at her back.

It would have to suffice.

"Your concern is almost touching, Miss Sutton." He strode forward, eliminating the distance separating them. "But then, I suppose any title-greedy viper would be similarly worried at the prospect of losing the lord she believes she has ensnared."

"Are you daring to insult me in my own family's establishment, my lord?"

"I speak truth." Curse it, was that her scent reaching him

just now? She smelled like a walk in a summer's meadow, fresh with a hint of a floral note.

East End fortune hunters were not meant to smell so luscious.

What the devil ails you? This is the woman Aidan has been chasing. And, knowing Aidan, bedding.

He disgusted himself. And yet, the woman before him possessed a certain attraction he could not deny. Not just her fine features or the vibrant warmth of her hair, but the manner in which she carried herself. He had no doubt, were she to stand in a ballroom, she would command the attention of every gentleman in the chamber.

"What truth do you speak, sir?" Her full lips compressed with disapproval.

Ah, a rarity, that. A woman who looked upon him as if he were disagreeable to behold. How intriguing. He could not recall the last time a lady had gazed at him with anything other than admiration, whether genuine or manufactured.

"That you are a title-greedy viper. It is to be expected of a lady in your unfortunate circumstances." He clenched his hands at his sides to keep from giving in to the urge to brush a stray wisp of hair from her cheek. "But I have come prepared to give you what you truly wish. How much do you require to leave my brother alone and end this nonsensical betrothal?"

Her eyes, a curious shade of green and gray with flecks of cinnamon, and fringed with generous lashes, widened. "Are you bribing me, my lord?"

"Yes," he said without hesitation. "I am."

"Ah." That lush mouth, which would have put any courtesan to shame, plumped into a pout. "I am afraid you are doomed to be disappointed. Suttons cannot be bought."

What was this utter nonsense? This complete lunacy she spouted? Of course baseborn families like hers could be bought. *Everyone* could be bought. And with ease. For the proper amount of coin, a gentleman could have anything he wanted. Did she think him a wet-behind-the-ears lad? Likely, she was attempting to do her utmost to secure a fat purse for herself and her misbegotten siblings. Yes, that was what she was doing, the greedy chit.

He tamped down a surge of ire, for it would not do to show a hint of emotion in this distasteful business.

"Everyone has a price," he countered smoothly, not at all dissuaded from his course. "Name yours."

"I cannot speak for everyone, my lord, but I can assure you that *I* haven't one."

Stubborn baggage. He could almost admire her determination. The defiant tilt to her chin briefly mesmerized him, accompanied by a shocking urge to place his lips there and discern whether or not the skin was as silken as he suspected.

Rot! He needed to get out of this damned stew.

"One hundred pounds," he offered, expecting he would need to bargain.

He wondered how many other third sons she had manipulated into marriage proposals before poor Aidan. Had she bedded them all? He could not resist studying her eyes, that rare indeterminate shade, curious over what secrets and stories hid behind them. And then he wondered why his brother had not simply made the lovely woman before him his mistress instead of deciding he must wed her. Heaven knew Aidan had kept any number of women before her; Garrick was not interested in his brother's prurient pursuits and had quite lost count.

The fault was Miss Sutton's, he suspected. Of course it was. Look at her. She was the personification of a goddess. Little wonder Aidan had fallen prey to her machinations. Lush curves which could not be hidden beneath her plain gown, a boldness which could not be denied, and hair that glinted in the candlelight.

Those magnificent lips moved. "No."

"Two hundred," he countered.

She moved past him then, striding forward in the calm, determined paces he would expect of a seasoned lady. But instead of skirting him, adhering to decorum and maintaining a distance between their persons, Miss Sutton passed by near enough that her upper arm brushed against his.

The sheer bravado of her. He might have been impressed were she any other woman on any other day.

His right arm was tingling with unwanted awareness, and he brushed it with his fingertips as he turned to face her. Garrick could only hope she would misconstrue the action as distaste for her lowly person connecting with his dearly expensive coat. As if she had perhaps left a stain instead of the haunting knowledge a female he had no right to find desirable had touched him there.

A fleeting touch, he reminded himself.

Scarcely anything.

She sat down at the desk and proceeded to ignore him.

To act as if he were not there.

It was a damned outrage.

He strode forward, determined to make the ill-bred minx pay for her rudeness. "For your insubordination, I am withdrawing five-and-twenty pounds from my previous offer. One hundred and seventy-five. I am afraid that is my final proposal. I have no doubt you were expecting more, but you shall not see it from me after such insolence."

"No," she said calmly and turned a page in the ledger. "Do you always spy upon the ledgers of the establishments you frequent, Lord Lordly?"

His nostrils flared as a strong bolt of irritation joined the unwanted attraction arcing through him. *By God,* the creature was intentionally mistaking his title. If her purpose was to nettle him, she had succeeded.

"Lord Lindsey, madam," he corrected grimly. "I will require an apology for the insults you have paid me, or I shall deduct another five-and-twenty pounds from my offer."

She remained seated, looking as imperious as a queen.

Except queen she was decidedly not. The woman was an East End lowborn fortune hunter, and he would not forget it, even if his brother was stupid enough not to know the difference.

She raised a brow. "Why should I apologize for any affront I have dealt when you have given me far more?"

"I have merely spoken truth, Miss Sutton. Do not dare to suggest to me that your attempt to manipulate my witless brother into matrimony is motivated by anything other than pure, cunning avarice."

She took up her quill and calmly made an entry in her ledger. "Lord Aidan is most certainly not witless."

Strangely, her championing of his idiotic sibling left Garrick feeling piqued. How foolish it was, envying Aidan this woman's loyalty when he knew it had its roots in greed. The only reason Miss Sutton had sunk her claws into him was to advance herself financially and socially.

She would find herself unable to do either.

Garrick tamped down the urge to snatch her pen from her fingers as she continued to make notations in her ledgers. "You will, at least, look at me whilst I am speaking to you, Miss Sutton."

She had the temerity to chuckle. "You may be the heir to a duke, but you don't own The Sinner's Palace, sir. I'll be doing as I please, and you can take yourself and your blustering elsewhere before I call on one of my brothers to drag your arse out of here."

Arse.

His *arse*?

He had never heard a lady utter such vile language in his presence before.

"How dare you threaten me?" he asked, determined the chit should get no more than one hundred pounds from him now.

At last, she glanced up, a slow grin curving her lips. "It ain't a threat, Lord Lordly."

Anger, white and pure and unstable, shot through him. Garrick's body was moving, propelled by a will of its own and the desire to accomplish the goal which had brought him here to this damnable impasse. He needed to persuade this creature that refusing to marry Aidan would benefit her far more than shackling herself to him for life ever could.

And yet, all the rational excuses and careful reasoning he had methodically planned *en route* to this temple of vice abandoned him as he stalked around the desk. If her shocked expression was any indication, he had taken Miss Sutton as much by surprise as himself. She hastened to stand, and that was when he made the unsettling discovery that the top of her head would fit neatly beneath his chin.

Not that he would ever have cause to place it there in such a tender embrace. Or an embrace at all. Amorous entanglements were of little interest to him. He had already chosen the woman he would wed, and he would not deign to sully her honor by cavorting in private with another. Many men did, and without compunction. Garrick had principles.

Those principles, however, were fast fading beneath the withering effect of the fury sparkling in Miss Sutton's hazel eyes. Her scent wound around him again, those untidy tendrils of hair which had escaped her coiffure confounding yet tempting. He lost his capacity for speech, the thunderous effect that her nearness had upon him so disconcerting, he could scarcely think.

What had he meant to say?

What was it about this woman, whom he had every reason to dislike and distrust?

She observed him without a hint of the admiration and fear he found so familiar amongst his own set, chin at a defiant angle. "And how dare *you* come into my family's gaming hell and accuse me of attempting to marry Aidan for his title or his fortune? I've enough coin of my own, and I certainly wouldn't want a bleeding title."

Something about her anger was rather glorious, and he could not discern precisely what. This was maddening. Vexing indeed.

He wanted to kiss her.

To press his lips to hers and test their softness, absorb their silken heat. There was something so lovely about kissing a woman—

"Well?" she asked, cutting through the silence and the absurdity of his thoughts both. "Have you nothing to say for yourself, my lord?"

He had to take his leave with as much haste as possible.

"Five hundred pounds," he said, desperation surpassing pride and the need to punish her both.

If he lingered in Miss Penelope Sutton's presence for much longer, he did not dare trust himself.

"If you think your money will excuse your appalling behavior, you are wrong." Her tone was filled with righteous ice.

Her daring and refusal to accept defeat was a potent lure. That was all, he was sure. A female refusing to defer to his reputation and title was an intriguing novelty. She would not otherwise interest him.

Aside from her undeniable loveliness, this woman had nothing at all to recommend her. And he would soon be betrothed to Lady Hester. This miscreant thought she could marry his brother.

"It is your behavior which is appalling, madam," he countered. "You cannot truly believe my brother will marry someone such as yourself."

"Is there a problem?"

The deep male voice, laden with a hint of suppressed menace, gave Garrick a start. The source of it—a tall, dark-haired gentleman clad in black—pinned him with a glare. Presumably one of Miss Sutton's siblings, then.

Garrick gave the man a terse nod. "No problem that cannot be solved. I am Lord Lindsey, brother to Lord Aidan Weir."

"I'm Hart Sutton," the interloper said coolly, yet offering him a bow, "brother to Pen here. We've ladies aplenty for your amusement, my lord. Pen doesn't sing any longer."

She sang? Why did the thought of her mellifluous voice raised in song unfurl a coil of heat deep within him?

"I have not come to hear her sing," he countered, careful to keep his voice calm and measured. There was no telling what manner of mischief the brigand before him would start. He was mired deep within a den of East End rogues and thieves. The very last place he had ever wished to find himself.

Blast you, Aidan.

"Why have you come then, my lord?" Hart Sutton asked, cocking his head in a manner that resembled his sister's commanding air. "If you are wanting a table, I would be more than pleased to see you settled."

"I do not gamble." He reserved that foolishness for his younger brother. "I have offered your sister five hundred pounds in exchange for her refusal to marry my brother. It is a handsome sum. I suggest you press her to consider my proposal, else I will have little recourse other than to make trouble for your establishment. I shall return in a day's time for my answer."

Garrick spied his chance for retreat.

He had already accomplished his main objective in providing Miss Penelope Sutton sufficient monetary reason to reconsider her greedy plans to ensnare his brother in matrimony. Lingering any longer would only prove as foolhardy as Aidan's reckless actions, and he was the eldest brother. The wise brother. The honorable one with an unimpeachable reputation.

Or, at least, he had been.

"Five hundred pounds?" Sutton's inky brows drew together in a perplexed frown. "Marriage? Pen, just what the devil is this bleeding fee, faw, fum?"

"An excellent question," Garrick said. "Your sister would be pleased to enlighten you, I am sure. I, however, am appallingly late for an engagement and must take my leave. I bid you both good evening."

Without bothering to glance in Miss Sutton's direction, he moved around the desk and strode across the small office from whence he had come.

"You needn't bother returning," she called after him.

But Garrick ignored her words of warning.

He would be back, and she *would* accept the five hundred pounds, curse her. There was no other recourse.

CHAPTER 2

Pen was *not* going to accept Lord Lordly's cursed five hundred pounds.

No.

Absolutely not.

Never.

There was not a chance she would allow the viscount to insult her honor and Aidan's by accepting his bribery. Aidan was her friend, and she owed him her loyalty. Despite his leather-headed notion they ought to marry, she would never dream of betraying him in such heartless fashion.

That his own brother would was appalling.

Why, suppose Aidan were in love with Pen. Would Lord Lordly truly wish to ruin his brother's future chance at happiness merely because he had deemed Pen unsuitable? Yes, she had no doubt he would. The man was arrogant and infuriating and insulting all at once. Hart ought to have given Lord Lordly a punch in his bread basket for his insults. Pen would have, had he lingered. And if he returned as he had warned, perhaps she would. It would certainly serve him right.

She paced down the length of the private room where she and her siblings—or those of them in residence at the hell these days, a dwindling number thanks to Jasper's marriage and Logan's disappearance—had gathered. Even Rafe was taking refuge in Mayfair for today.

"He can take his coin and shove it up his—"

"Now, now, Pen," interrupted Hart with a pointed glance in their younger sister Lily's direction. "*The child* is listening."

"I was going to say nose," she grumbled.

"Cease calling me that," Lily snapped, pinning their brother with an irritated glare. "I haven't been a child in years. I'm old enough to wed."

"No," their other brother Wolf said, "you're not."

"I am a woman, and blast you all for insisting upon treating me as if I were the baby of the family." Lily sniffed.

"You *are* the bleeding baby of the family, Lil. You're the youngest of us all," Wolf pointed out.

"I'll give any cove sniffing about your skirts the basting of his life," Hart added.

Pen sighed. Their brothers were protective. From their eldest brother, Jasper, to Rafe, and then Hart and Wolf, a Sutton lady could scarcely take a breath about a gentleman without fear her brothers would give him a drubbing and warn him away. Heavens knew Rafe had done so to Aidan. But Aidan was her friend, just as he had always been, even if he had ignored her irate summons in the wake of his older brother's unexpected call. He could not ignore her forever. And besides all that, her brother's concern had been misguided.

Every bit as misguided as Aidan's own brother's was now.

Just thinking of the arrogant lord who had paid an unexpected call upon her the evening before had a queer flare of awareness lighting within her. It was the same feeling she'd had once before, the one she had followed to her detriment.

But Daniel had no place in her worries now. He was decidedly in the past, where he belonged, and where he would forever remain.

And the present was laden with problems enough of its own. Old problems could remain where they were, long since buried.

"If the three of you would cease squabbling," she said, turning her attention to her siblings, "perhaps we might discuss the viscount's threat to return this evening."

After his departure the night before, an unexpected melee had occurred in the gaming quarters, spurred by an argument over a mistress between two drunken lords. Mayhem had been narrowly circumvented by Hart expertly calming the soaring tempers. With Hart and Wolf watching the floor closely for the rest of the evening, Pen hadn't had the opportunity to speak with her brothers about Lord Lindsey's unexpected appearance and subsequent attempt to bribe her.

"When do you suppose hisnabs is going to arrive?" Hart asked, stroking his jaw with a contemplative air.

"Five hundred pounds, you say?" Wolf grinned. "I'll be 'appy to accept it for you."

"Will you not take this seriously?" she demanded. "I fear Lord Lindsey will cause problems for The Sinner's Palace if I do not take his bloody coin and do as he has ordered me. He threatened as much last night before leaving."

"Then take the damned coin," Lily suggested. "Lord Aidan is a troublesome cove, and we don't need more than we've already got, what with the Bradleys and the fire."

The Bradley family, owners of a rival gaming hell in the East End, had been causing the devil's own stir. But it had been their eldest brother Jasper who had unwittingly brought more destruction down upon them when the East End property for their new gaming hell had been set aflame by a madwoman from his past.

"There must be a different solution," she said, frowning at her sister.

"You don't want to marry Lord Aidan anyhow," Hart said, agreeing with Lily. "You said as much last night. You may as well take the coin and be richer for all the grief Lord Aidan has caused."

Why did everyone always blame Aidan? He was of an age with Pen, a charming rascal who never failed to make her laugh. The two of them had been unlikely—though fast—friends ever since she had made his acquaintance here at the hell. From their first meeting, Aidan had made a habit of sneaking into the private quarters and regaling her with tales of his antics. He had also indulged the sense of adventure her overbearing brothers had sought to quell.

"While it's true that I am not marrying Lord Aidan, he has not caused any grief," she defended her friend.

His reputation preceded him. For the entirety of their friendship, Pen's family had been warning her away from him and telling her he was a n'er-do-well best ignored. And yet, no one knew him as she did. His mischievous nature had never extended to her.

At least, not until he had announced his intention to marry her, all as a sport to infuriate his family, with whom he was currently displeased. Pen had no wish to be the sword he used to fight them, however.

"Setting his arrogant lordling brother upon us ain't causing grief?" Wolf crossed his arms over his chest, his disdain for the quality showing.

"Aidan hardly asked the viscount to come here and browbeat me." Pen shot her brother a chastising glare. "He would not intentionally do any harm to us or The Sinner's Palace."

"You never did say why the whelp is running about announcing your betrothal." Hart's eyes narrowed. "There ain't a chance of Lindsey or old Dryden allowing their precious blood to mingle with a Sutton's, and the empty-headed shite ought to know it."

"Please stop insulting my friend." It was Pen's turn to cross her arms over her chest.

Perhaps coming to her siblings with this problem had been a mistake. None of them seemed ready to provide a resolution, and instead, Aidan was the recipient of a verbal thrashing. Not that she could entirely blame Hart. Pen herself had been quite outraged when she had realized Aidan had ignored her polite refusal of his suggestion and had taken the nonsensical announcement to his family.

Now she was left to deal with the repercussions.

"He ain't your friend, or he would be here when his dog of a brother turns up snarling, with bared teeth," Wolf said coolly.

While she had not seen or heard from Aidan since she had told him she would not agree to his madcap plan of marriage, that was hardly unusual. Aidan was like the wind. He blew about wherever he wished, and he was often easily distracted by whatever amusements were before him at the moment. He had been rather vexed with her when he had taken his leave as well, and she had supposed he may have been hurt by her refusal.

However, regardless of his feelings, it was apparent he had proceeded with his plan. And despite her wishes to the contrary. Her fondness for Aidan aside, Pen still intended to harangue him when he reappeared for causing her such headaches. Perhaps even box his ears...

"I didn't gather you all so you could insult poor Aidan," she said, despite her own less-than-generous thoughts concerning him. "I wanted your opinions on what I should do about his brother, should he return this evening."

"We already told you," Wolf said, shaking his head as if

she were a lost cause. "Take the coin and forget about the cove."

"Less trouble is what we need," Hart added.

"Especially after the fire," offered Lily.

Pen sighed. This was not the advice she had wished to hear. It was, however, what she had feared. "Very well. I shall see to his high and mighty lordship myself when he returns."

"That one's starched," Wolf observed. "Don't think you'll need much help from us. But we'll be about, and so will the lads."

By the lads, he meant the many hulking guards The Sinner's Palace employed for the protection of not just their patrons, but the Sutton family themselves. Those men were as trusted as family members and hardly what one would think of as lads.

"Take the coin," Hart added grimly, "and do what's best for us all."

A sigh of disappointment escaped Pen, for accepting Lord Lordly's bribe was not at all what she wished to do. There had to be another way to appease him. Or to persuade him she had no desire to marry his brother.

Or merely to chase him away so that he might never return.

Chasing him away? Ah, yes. There was the better choice. Perhaps the sole one.

All she required was a plan.

His eagerness to be rid of the dreadful Miss Penelope Sutton drove Garrick to The Sinner's Palace earlier than he had planned. That, and his mother having requested an audience with him. Rather than listen to Mama prattle on about Lady Hester's reputation and suitability as the future

Duchess of Dryden, he had sent her a note explaining he would be settling the matter of her youngest son's regrettable decision to attempt to shackle himself to a beautiful fortune-hunting harlot.

In so many words.

Naturally, Garrick had employed no small amount of tact in his reply. His reputation for being society's most proper gentleman had not been earned through mere gossip. He did his utmost to be the embodiment of propriety and well-bred manners. Which meant that he refrained from referring to Miss Sutton as beautiful, and he avoided calling her a harlot.

As his conveyance pulled to a halt at the rear of The Sinner's Palace, Garrick adjusted the fit of his gloves and the tilt of his hat before smoothing a slight wrinkle from his great coat. Perfection pleased him. Anything less was cause for not just dismay, but aggravation.

Garrick disliked aggravation immensely.

It made his eye twitch.

In his customary habit, he tugged at his left coat sleeve first and then his right coat sleeve before disembarking. There were two massive fellows flanking the private entrance to the Sutton family gaming hell today. The air was cold with the portent of rain. In addition to aggravation, Garrick also found most precipitation grievously displeasing. Snow, on occasion, was acceptable enough. But only in moderate amounts in the country, and for approximately ten minutes.

He approached the guards, deciding to pretend as if they were footmen rather than hulking East End scoundrels. Doing so certainly lent a less distasteful air to this entire sordid affair. "Viscount Lindsey to see Miss Sutton."

"Which Miss Sutton is it?" asked the man on the right, looking distinctly unimpressed.

There was more than one? *Christ.*

"Miss Penelope Sutton," he elaborated, stifling a sigh of irritation. "She will be expecting me."

"She ain't 'ere," said the fellow on the left, crossing his arms over his chest.

This was an unexpected development. And a vexing one at that.

He frowned, for he was early, it was true. But curse the woman, he had warned her he would return. "Where has she gone?"

"Don't know." The man made a snorting sound, as if he were inhaling something unsavory.

Perhaps snot.

Garrick took a step in retreat, hoping the giant in question did not have anything that was catching. "Did Miss Sutton say when she might be returning?"

The man took his time responding, making a wretched sound deep in his throat that must have somehow been related to the snot. "No."

Garrick waited for one of the pair to offer something more. Instead, they simply remained firm in their stances and stony-eyed silence. Did they not know who he was?

"Perhaps you have never heard my name," he said, though the admission was irritating indeed. "I am the heir to the Duke of Dryden. My good opinion is quite highly regarded in the *ton*."

The man on the right shrugged.

The man on the left remained as still as a marble bust.

Where the devil was the lad whose palms he had greased the day before? Finding his way into the inner sanctum of The Sinner's Palace had proven much easier yesterday.

He looked from one unimpressed guard to the other. Neither man blinked or moved.

He cleared his throat and tried again. "I will await Miss Sutton's return."

"Don't think Miss Sutton'd like that, milord," said the one on the right.

Perhaps not.

He smiled for the first time since his arrival in this godforsaken place. "Whether or not Miss Sutton likes it is immaterial."

"Entrance for the nobs is in front," added the guard with the apparent nasal problem, making another snorting sound, as if to punctuate his instruction.

It was utterly impossible to fathom why this dung pile was so cursed popular with all the dandies, fops, and bucks. Gambling and drink would blind a man to anything, he supposed. Fortunately, Garrick had never found himself afflicted with either sin.

"I have come specifically to speak with Miss Sutton," he countered calmly. "I have no desire to wait about in a gaming hall."

"As you like, milord." The guard on the right offered a shrug.

They truly intended to deny him entrance?

His nostrils flared. This was outrageous. An egregious affront.

Miss Sutton was going to pay dearly for this most recent slight.

"Perhaps I can offer the two of you some remuneration in return for your reconsideration," he suggested through gritted teeth.

"Suttons pay well enough," said the man on the left.

"Our loyalty is to them," added the man on the right.

"Then if one of you could be kind enough to inquire within as to whether or not Miss Sutton has returned?" he tried next, his patience waning.

He was beginning to suspect this entire tableau had been

orchestrated by his brother's fortune-seeking betrothed. Was the minx truly wily enough?

"Would you be wanting to go inside and inquire, Randall?" the one on the left asked the other.

"Don't think so," said the right guard. Randall, apparently. "Why don't you?"

"Don't want to," said the other.

This was all Aidan's fault. Him and his stupidity, following his blind lust all the way to this stew. Mother's frantic words returned to him as he waited. *It will be the mésalliance of the century, Lindsey. We shall be the laughingstock of society.*

Yes, yes, he had to put an end to this damned farce.

Today.

He straightened his shoulders and pinned the guards with his most contemptuous glare. "I demand you to allow me entrance. You cannot expect me to wait about in the street. I refuse to accept such an insult."

Before either of the men could answer, the door they were so assiduously guarding opened to reveal none other than Miss Penelope Sutton. And she was grinning, damn her, as if she had been witnessing this entire affair with glee.

She probably had.

"Lord Lordly," she greeted him with insolence, confirming his suspicion. "What brings you to The Sinner's Palace?"

His lip curled, but he did not bother to correct her, though her obfuscation of his title was infuriating. "You know the reason, Miss Sutton."

"I am afraid I am in the midst of some pressing business," she said blithely, "but you may await me in the parlor."

Parlor.

Of course they would have a parlor in a wretched little heap like this, rather than a drawing room. What had he expected? Still, the prospect of awaiting her in some dingy little box as he had done the night before set his teeth on edge.

"I have already wasted a considerable amount of my time here at this door," he pointed out, sending a pointed glare in the direction of her guards for good measure.

"Hugh and Randall, please see his lordship settled in the parlor," she directed the guards as if he had not just offered his objection to her plan. "I will be with you as soon as I am able."

Before he could offer protest, Miss Sutton turned and disappeared.

The woman grew more outrageous, more utterly insulting and infuriating by the moment. It was more than clear to him that she was playing a game she believed she would emerge from as the victor.

Ha!

She had never met anyone as determined as he. Garrick would be willing to wager his very life upon it.

CHAPTER 3

"How long has his lordship been waiting in the parlor, Hugh?" Pen asked for what must have been the fifth time since she had sent Aidan's brother there to await her.

Yes, it had been with the intention that he should remain there for a prolonged period of time. Until he surrendered in this little war of theirs and returned home, conceding defeat. However, she had not expected the arrogant devil's patience to last this long.

"One and one quarter hour, Miss Sutton," the guard reported. "The cove's a mite caged by now."

"Sulking, is he?" Pen knew a queer mixture of gratification and guilt at the revelation that Lord Lordly was vexed with her for making him wait.

And wait.

And *wait.*

She could not contain the smile of satisfaction that turned up her lips at the thought of him pacing the small confines of the parlor, outraged that she had yet to appear.

"Asked for chatter broth instead of brandy 'e did. Deuced odd cull." Hugh shook his head.

She tried to imagine the viscount sipping at his tea utterly alone, all aloof and proper, as if he were holding court with a bevy of admirers. The thought made her guilt heighten, chasing the fleeting sense of victory and her smile both.

Pen sighed. "Has he expressed his frustration?"

"Strangest thing, but 'e ain't upset at all." Hugh shrugged. "Unless the nob's grumbling in the gizzard."

Hmm.

The notion that Lord Lordly was hiding his dismay and irritation was...shocking. Indeed, it stole the already waning remnants of her enjoyment. She had many duties awaiting her today. In addition to keeping the ledgers for The Sinner's Palace, Pen was also aiding in the preparations for a new gaming hell she and her siblings were planning to open in the West End to replace the hell which had been destroyed by fire.

She had many tasks awaiting her attention, and the longer Lord Lordly stayed in the parlor, sipping his tea, the less time she would have to accomplish them.

"Thank you, Hugh," she said, deciding it was time to try a new tactic where the aggravating viscount was concerned. "I suppose I must speak with him or I'll never see a thing done today."

"Any other way I can be of service?" Hugh asked, ever the loyal retainer.

"Not for now, no," she said, knowing she needed to face the viscount and his assumptions and his arrogance and his insults and his bribery.

Alone.

She scarcely suppressed the shiver that wanted to dance down her spine as she took her leave of the office and made a hasty path to the parlor. It was not that she was afraid of his lordship. Not at all. But she could not like the manner in which he had suggested he would cause problems for her family.

Her siblings had not been wrong.

They had faced enough adversity, danger, trouble, and damage in their lives. She would not willingly be the source for more.

If only Aidan would have answered me. He can easily disabuse his insufferable brother of the idea that I agreed to marry him.

But Aidan was avoiding her. Ignoring her missives. The lad she had sent round to his common haunts had returned without a hint of where her friend could have gone. Which meant that either he had immersed himself in the pleasures at The Garden of Flora or he was intentionally eluding Pen. The Garden of Flora was London's most sought-after School of Venus, and Aidan had been known to spend several days at a time within its walls without emerging, indulging in only he knew what manner of licentiousness. Yet another reason why Lord Aidan Weir was not a man she would ever agree to wed.

He was a delightful friend to have—when he was not running about attempting to use her to infuriate his family, of course. He was loyal, never failed to make her laugh, and he had not blinked an eye at her request to be her escort at the bare-knuckle boxing matches she dearly longed to attend. But he was easily distracted, a dreadful rakehell, and he was infamously unreliable in moments when it mattered most.

Moments such as this one.

Here.

Now.

Pen opened the door to the parlor and strode over the threshold, telling herself she would not be cowed by Lord

Lordly. But the moment she entered the chamber and found herself alone with him, everything changed.

He was not seated and sipping his tea as she had expected him to be. Instead, he was standing. Aidan was tall, but the viscount possessed a different sort of stature altogether from his younger brother. His stiff posture, broad shoulders, and impressive height united to create the impression that he did not just dominate the room.

He *was* the room.

His form, all large, lean, muscled strength, was impressive. Imperious.

Breath stealing.

Breath stealing?

What in the devil's arsehole was wrong with her? And since when had she begun to use her brother Rafe's epithets? This was a problem. Lord Lordly was a problem. Aidan's refusal to correct his error was a problem.

She was adrift in a sea of them, it would seem.

The viscount offered her a bow that was nothing short of magnificent. She fancied he must have practiced it at least a hundred times to embody such a graceful flow of perfection. She had never seen a man move with his easy elegance, particularly not a gentleman of his size.

"Miss Sutton," he said, his voice low and smooth and strangely silken.

Heat flared to life deep within her.

She ruthlessly quelled it, dipping into the barest of curtseys, for she was not a woman who gave a damn about the quality or their nonsensical adherence to manners. "Lord Lordly."

Although she ought to have resisted goading him, she could not seem to help herself where this man was concerned.

His eyes narrowed the slightest hint. They were icy and blue, a most striking hue. "I have the funds at the ready."

The five hundred pounds. Of course.

Her heart beat faster. She had been shamelessly taking in the sight of his lordship, noting how handsome and strong he was, whilst he was concerning himself with how he might sufficiently pay her to keep her from sullying his precious and hallowed family. The son of a duke could never marry a lowly born East End girl like her.

It was wrong to admire the formidable slash of his jaw and the chiseled outline of his lips. It was also terrible of her to appreciate the sweep of his dark hair, the perfect manner in which it was cropped and sleek and shining. How *did* he manage such lustrous locks? Hers were dreadfully dull by comparison. Undoubtedly, it was something he achieved by nefarious means, such as drinking the blood of virgins on the first full moon of the year.

That is rather uncharitable of me.

I should be polite.

This man could cause all manner of problems for my family.

There was the voice of reason rising within the shadowy corners of her mind, the one she often ignored. And yet, his insistence upon remaining, coupled with his lovely face, and those ice-blue eyes, why, he managed to affect her in a way no man had since…

Nay!

She struck the thought from her mind and forced herself back to the problem awaiting her. The handsome, lordly, haughty problem.

"I have already told you that I've no intention of accepting your bribe," she said, and then cursed herself for her stubborn sense of pride.

For she was misleading him. Quite likely, he believed she was determined to hold on to her supposed betrothal to

Aidan, when in truth she was desperate for the opposite. There was no betrothal as far as she was concerned. Oh, what a hopeless muddle.

"Just who do you think you are, my dear?" Slowly, with elegant and graceful deliberation, Lord Lindsey moved toward her. Prowling in the way only a duke's heir truly could. "Could you possibly be foolish enough to suppose you have the ability to refuse me?"

Had she thought him handsome? Surely it had been a trick of the light.

Clinging to her outrage, she met him halfway across the small, woefully decorated parlor. It was a dusty chamber, frequently unused as she and her siblings inevitably preferred to dwell in other areas of the establishment that felt less...proper and stifling. She hoped Lord Lordly had spent his time within these walls sneezing.

She stopped just short of his booted toes, holding his gaze as defiance thundered through her. "I'll not accept your blood money, my lord. Save it for someone else who will be easily bought. I'm a Sutton, and we are loyal."

The corner of the viscount's mouth lifted in a half smirk. "Loyal to your greed and your determination to rise above your station, you mean."

"Loyal to those who deserve our loyalty," she corrected coldly, wondering what it must be like to possess such a disillusioned view of those around him. "Loyal to those who have earned it."

Had Aidan earned hers? She was beginning to wonder. This troublesome business with his brother was far more than she had bargained for, and his sudden absence was as alarming as his apparent betrothal announcement to his family was. How dare he use her in such fashion? For surely, there was no other means by which she might describe his recent actions.

But that was another problem for another day. For now, today's vexation was towering over her, exuding a cold conceit that chilled her to the marrow and yet heated some strange part of her all at once.

He bit out a laugh that was steeped in mockery, lips twisting in a smile to match. "Allow me to see if I understand you, Miss Sutton. You are suggesting that you are refusing my more-than-generous offer to forego marrying my idiotic brother out of some sense of loyalty, rather than greed. Is that it?"

"Yes," she said with a nod, "it is."

Only, when he said it thus, he made her motives sound suspect. What a bitter, distrusting man he was. What could have happened to make him thus? Aidan, for all his faults, was always ready with an easy laugh and a genuine smile. He did not ridicule or cling to his position in society.

"Ha," said the viscount, nary a hint of levity in him.

Why wait to box Aidan's ears? Perhaps she might begin with his brother.

Pen sighed. "Am I meant to suppose you do not believe me? I fear that false ducal laughter is not easily translated."

"Hmm."

His gaze was searching, his tone and his expression both rife with disapproval.

"That's all you 'ave to say, Lord Lordly?" she asked, omitting her *h* just to spite him.

Jasper had known there would be value in them all speaking well. From the time money had permitted, he had seen them all educated. For some of her older siblings, slipping into flash was more familiar than it was for Pen, though she was still plagued by the occasional lapse. Lord Lordly needn't know that, however. Let him stew, thinking about how horrific it would be for his younger brother to marry a lowborn lady who could not even mimic her betters.

"I am not a duke."

Of all the things he might have said, somehow, this response surprised Pen most. "Yet."

He inclined his head. "I hope to remain Lord Lindsey for many, many years."

He would only become the duke when his father died, his sober expression and his words reminded her. But he was ducal enough on his own. What a strange life it must be for the quality. Oddly, she had never considered it before, over the course of her friendship with Aidan. He had always merely been someone who agreed to all her larks and humored her every wish. All this, he had done with a charming—and sometimes drunken—grin.

She nodded. "Of course. I did not mean to suggest you are awaiting the death of your father. To do so would be dreadfully insulting. Rather in the vein of someone suggesting a lady wished to marry her friend solely for his fortune and familial connections."

Her words were as pointed as any blade, and if she were to judge from the viscount's countenance, she would wager they had hit their mark.

His jaw tensed. "I find myself growing weary of this aimless prattle, Miss Sutton. Let me be clear. You will accept the five hundred pounds I am willing to generously offer you. It is a king's ransom and far more than marriage to Aidan is worth. In return, you will end your betrothal with my brother and forego all further communication with him. Indeed, you will cut him from your life altogether from this moment forward."

His absolute belief that she would accept his edict rankled.

"Did you ever stop to suppose that your brother and I are in love?" she asked, frustrated with his condescension. "Or had it never occurred to you that Aidan might be hopelessly besotted with me and that your bribery, should I accept it, would break his heart?"

His lordship flashed her a thin, condescending smile. "He would have no trouble nursing his wounded heart at the nearest brothel. Which begs the question, Miss Sutton, of whether or not you have considered the man with whom you have pledged your troth. Aidan is nothing if not inconstant. If he has told you he loves you, it is only because he has yet to find a lovelier, brighter, more generous-breasted version of yourself upon whom he might ply his flattery."

She ought to slap the viscount for his insult. But the truth was, he was not entirely wrong in his estimation of Aidan. She knew he was fickle and faithless in romance, which was why they made excellent friends and one of many reasons why she would never marry him.

And there was something so very dismaying and disheartening in Lord Lindsey's words. He was not an unintelligent man; quite the opposite. His was a rare, cutting understanding of the world around him. Bitter and jaded, yet somehow grounded in more than a modicum of truth, despite his cynicism.

"You do not like your own brother," she said, an astonishing realization to make not just because she cared for Aidan as if he were another brother, but because she also loved each of her siblings. She would do anything for them, just as she knew each of them would lay down their lives to protect hers.

But then, as she had already told Lord Lordly, Suttons were loyal, a trait it would seem the Weir family did not possess.

"I dislike the problems he is intent upon causing for our family by expressing his desire to marry an unsuitable fortune-hunter," he corrected coolly, watching her with such unflappable calm that he might not have been speaking of her at all.

Except, he was. And he was insulting her yet again. Why, it was fortunate indeed for Viscount Lindsey that he was so pleasant to look upon, for the moment he opened his mouth, he was rendered altogether disagreeable. If he were to just stand in the corner, looking handsome and masculine and ducal without uttering a word, it would suit Pen just fine.

"I am not a fortune hunter," she ground out, her denial stinging. "And Aidan is due far more respect than you have shown him. He may be a devil-may-care but he ain't a bad cove. His heart is good."

He was just occasionally misguided and reckless.

Perhaps more than occasionally.

But never mind that. Lord Lordly had no right to disparage him so!

The viscount's icy gaze searched hers. "You expect me to believe that you are hopelessly in love with my brother and that you are not merely manipulating him into forming one of the worst mésalliances of the century because you are hungry for his money and his familial connections. Is that not correct?"

Agreeing would be disingenuous.

"I never said I was hopelessly in love with him," she pointed out.

"Ah. There we have it. The truth at last."

His grim pronouncement nettled her. "You are deliberately misunderstanding me, my lord."

"Am I?" A new, contemptuous smile pulled the corners of his aristocratic mouth upward.

"Yes, curse you." Her fingers curled into her palms in impotent outrage. She did not think she had ever been so vexed with another person in her life.

He surprised her by taking another step closer, bringing

their bodies flush. Although he did not touch Pen, he may as well have with the effect his sudden nearness was having upon her.

"Shall I prove just how right I am about you, Miss Sutton?" he asked, his deep voice losing some of its ice.

There was something about the abrupt shift in his rich baritone that held her briefly spellbound. When he was not at his most cutting, Lord Lordly was capable of impressive charm. She could almost allow herself to become lost in the depths of his eyes, to admire his rigid jaw, cleanly shaven but already with the hint of whiskers shadowing the masculine angle. Or to become distracted by the temptation of his mouth.

Fortunately, she was made of sterner stuff, and having been bamboozled by a handsome rogue once before, she would never allow herself to be so swindled again.

She tipped back her chin in defiance, refusing to retreat. "Please do, Lord Lordly."

After all, there was no means by which he could prove she was an avaricious fortune hunter. She did not even want to marry Aidan. Or anyone.

"With pleasure," he said smoothly.

And then his high and mighty lordship did something else that was cause for further astonishment. He slid an arm around her waist and drew her into his tall, imperious frame. Gently and slowly, giving her ample opportunity to object. Fool that she was, Pen found herself melting against him, the weakest part of her nature reveling in the heat and strength he exuded. A swift inhalation of shock provided another element of teasing to her senses. He smelled of citrus and bay and musk. Fresh and crisp and expensive and lordly.

Of course he did.

His head dipped, his handsome face drawing nearer to hers.

He was going to kiss her.

Good heavens, this entitled, arrogant lord intended to put his mouth on hers.

She could object. She *should* object.

She was not going to. Her hands, which had been largely idle at her sides during the course of their conversation, moved to his shoulders. Her fingers uncurled, resting lightly on the expensive wool of his coat.

He could kiss her all he liked. She would remain unmoved. She was sure she would feel absolutely nothing for this conceited…

His mouth was hot. Hesitant. The barest brush of those smirking patrician lips over hers. Once. Twice. *Oh dear.* Something stranger still happened. A fluttery sensation started low in her belly. Heat bloomed everywhere.

And Pen's arms slid around his neck, pulling him closer as her mouth responded to his.

~

MISTAKE.

This was a mistake. A terrible, egregious, despicable one. Had he not learned his lesson years ago with Veronica? What was he doing?

His mind was galloping faster than a runaway horse, trying to warn him of all the reasons why he ought to put an end to his impulsive decision to demonstrate to the both of them that she was not in love with Aidan. That there was only one reason she wanted to marry his brother, and it was the lure of a wealthy lord on her arm.

Garrick never should have kissed her. The first touch of his mouth to hers had lit a spark within him that was suddenly an uncontrollable fire. He had to have more, regardless of how foolish and idiotic and wrong this all was.

Miss Sutton was in his arms, her soft, supple curves pressed against him in all the right places. And suddenly *she* was the one kissing *him*, those lush siren's lips clinging to his as if she could not possibly have enough. It was the single most erotic moment of his life, and he had absolutely no control over his body's instinctive reaction.

His cockstand was instant.

Mistake, cautioned that same voice in his mind again, the one which had inevitably led to him making the right decisions in every instance of turmoil. Only, in this instance, it was being dulled and drowned by the thud of his pulse and the roaring need rising to the surface.

And still, he could not seem to cease this madness.

All he could do was surrender to the moment, to the desire. He forgot who she was, why he must not be kissing her, why he had come here. Her breasts were heavy and full, crushed against his chest. Her floral scent curled around him. He lost himself in the silken luxury of her mouth. Garrick had never dreamt a lady's lips could be so sinfully smooth and hot. He had spent years of penance eschewing vice, but here was one he could easily lose himself in: this woman.

God, she felt good in his arms, good with her curves blending into his hardness. Good in every way that mattered and all the ones that did not, too. He could not resist tasting her. His tongue slipped into the velvet heat of her mouth. She tasted impossibly sweet, like honey cakes with a hint of sin.

Sin because this was wrong.

Yet right.

And he had ever been drawn to temptation, wretched sinner that he was.

She made a sound of need, her fingers tightening on his shoulders, the dainty tips digging into his muscle and holding him close. Her lips and tongue moved in a sinuous dance, leaving him aching with want.

More. He had to have more. Garrick did not partake in spirits, but suddenly, he understood the lure. Kissing Penelope Sutton was intoxicating. Little wonder Aidan was so enamored of her…

Oh, bloody hell.

Aidan.

The reminder of his brother was enough to force Garrick to tear himself from Miss Sutton. His lips tingled with the memory of hers, and damn the worst part of him to perdition for taking note of that lush mouth, dark and swollen from his kiss. Damn the gratification that rose.

He should be disgusted with himself.

He *was* disgusted.

Had she kissed his brother with such passion?

He would have asked, but his fear of the answer and the resulting self-hatred was an ever-swelling tide.

She was still holding on to him as if he were necessary to keeping her standing upright. And he knew the feeling. It was as if a sudden, violent storm had passed through his landscape. Everything had changed inside him with confusing, blistering force. Yet, everything was the same.

Why had he kissed her?

To prove she is a fortune-hunting harlot.

Ah, yes. That was the reason.

If only his body would recall the course his mind had chosen for them.

Garrick summoned a cold smile, intending to show her just how impervious he was to their kisses. "I have proven the truth now, have I not? If you wanted to marry Aidan because you are hopelessly in love with him, I can scarcely imagine you would have reacted to his own brother with such improper lewdness."

A flush rose to her cheeks and she flinched away from him as if he had struck her. "How do you dare?"

He mourned the loss of her touch. His stupid, weak body ached for her generous breasts to be molded to his chest. He felt certain she was not wearing stays beneath that gown and that he had known for the briefest, most wondrous of moments, the prod of her hard little nipples against his coat.

He swallowed down an inconvenient rush of lust. "The true question, madam, is how *you* dare? How do you dare to kiss the brother of the man you profess to love? You ought to be ashamed."

In truth, Garrick ought to be ashamed as well, and he knew it. But allowing Miss Sutton to know he experienced even a moment of guilt—or any emotion at all, for that matter—over what had just happened between them was more than his pride could endure. He had already brought himself pathetically low.

He was despicable.

Miss Sutton's brow rose and her nostrils flared, the naked passion on her lovely face vanishing. In its stead was a cool, rigid expression of understanding. "Do not pretend you kissed me to prove yourself, Lord Lordly."

He did not like what she was suggesting. "Of course I did."

She shook her head, a slight, knowing smile lifting her lips. "You kissed me because you wanted to."

His ears were suddenly overly hot, and the most disagreeable prickling sensation began on the skin of his face. "I did nothing of the sort."

"Yes, you did," the bold baggage insisted, "and you liked it, too."

Of course he had.

Garrick straightened his shoulders, summoning his most frigid expression, the one which could utterly destroy anyone in polite society. "Of course I did not."

Her hazel gaze traveled over his anatomy in troubling, familiar fashion, lingering on the part of him that proved him every bit as much a liar as she was. "Then how do you explain your cockstand?"

He thought he may have swallowed his tongue. How incredibly common of her to give voice to the unspeakable. No lady in his acquaintance would have dared to be so familiar. But then, as he had already established repeatedly and with the brilliance of the burning sun, Penelope Sutton was no lady.

"Your effrontery astounds me, madam," he bit out coldly.

She cast a pointed glance down his body. "Yes, you do appear rather…*astounded,* Lord Lordly."

She dared to taunt him now, after she had just kissed him with the practiced ease of a trollop when she was betrothed to his brother? To say nothing of the appalling manner in which she had referred to his distressing state. *Repeatedly.*

"Once again, you prove just how unsuitable you are," he said, wishing he felt a modicum of the satisfaction he ought. "You may rest assured that I will be taking the tale of what happened between us here today to Aidan. After he realizes your true nature, I doubt he would even want you. I must thank you for solving my problem for me, and without the need to lose a fortune."

Instead of being pleased that she had aided him to her doom, however, all Garrick felt was a hollow sense of disappointment. It was almost as if part of him had hoped she would indeed prove him wrong. He also could not seem to control the effect she had on him. He wanted her.

He could not deny it.

But he also could not have her.

He was going to be taking a wife of his own soon, and he had parted ways with his last mistress in respect to Lady Hester. He most certainly would not take another now, and most certainly not *her*. What the devil was the matter with him? Specifically with *that* part of him? His manhood had never so betrayed him in the past.

Nor had he ever responded so intensely to another, however, either. Not even Veronica. It was an unfathomable, uncomfortable revelation.

"If you have achieved the outcome you sought, then I suggest you be on your way," she said, her curt voice cutting into his wildly racing thoughts.

He had, had he not?

Why did this victory feel as sharp as a blade, inserted between his ribs?

He inclined his head, clinging to his stoic bearing since all else—including ration and reason—had fled him. "I have indeed. I bid you good day, Miss Sutton."

With an abbreviated bow, he stalked away from her, at long last taking his leave of this den of Satan. His steps could not carry him away with enough haste. Back to Mayfair where he belonged.

He would banish Penelope Sutton and the feeling of her lips beneath his from his mind and never again think her name.

CHAPTER 4

If any of her siblings knew what she was about, Pen had no doubt they would be furious. Livid. Utterly outraged. But what Sutton brothers and sisters did not know could never hurt them. She had been living firmly by that credo for as long as she could recall.

"You will wait for me, yes?" she asked the driver of the hack she had hired to bring her to her secret destination. "There will be a great deal more coin for you upon my return. All you need to do is wait. I shan't be long."

"Aye." The fellow leered at her. "I knows what you'll be doing within."

She sighed. "No, you don't. I'm paying you handsomely."

His grin deepened. "Aye, that you be."

Lingering and arguing her case was futile, she could already see. The man would believe what he wished, which was that she was entering the edifice before them so she could indulge in whatever Cyrenaic delights awaited her within. Eh, if it pleased him to think so, what was the harm? It was not as if she were a fine lady with a reputation to preserve. Nor was it as if she were the betrothed of a lord. Rather, she was someone Viscount Lindsey deemed worthy of bribery and cruel kisses only.

Yes, that rather still stung, his disdainful reaction to those shared moments of what had been, for her, nothing short of wondrous. Apparently, for Lord Lordly, it had all been the means to an end. She hoped he was pleased with himself. If nothing else, it had rid her of his dogged persistence and unwanted presence. Very likely, he was somewhere in Mayfair, casting a disagreeable pall upon some silly ball or musicale.

"I will return in one quarter hour," she reminded the hackney driver.

He nodded his ascent, and she turned with a sigh to approach the small, secret entrance to The Garden of Flora. It was a door she had visited on a few occasions previously, always with Aidan. Had any of her family known she had been within the brothel…

Well, no need to fret over what they would do to Aidan now.

Because she was searching for him. She had not seen him in days, and nor had he answered any of the notes she had sent round to him. It was the first time in their acquaintance when he had ever allowed so much time to pass without contacting her in some fashion. And although she knew he was aware of how outraged she was with him for his machinations, she nevertheless had been unable to quell her steadily rising fear that something ill had befallen him.

Thus had begun a second, more thorough search of all his haunts.

Nary a hint of him in any of the taverns or hells or even his bachelor residence, those shabby rooms he kept just so that he might escape the domineering rule of his family. And good heavens, now that she had met Lord Lordly, she could scarcely blame her friend for the desire to flee.

But all that aside, there were only so many places Aidan could be, and Pen had visited them all. All of them, anyway, save this one.

She reached the door and knocked.

A moment later, the tiny slat cut into the door itself opened, revealing a pair of eyes and no more. "What is it you wish, madam?"

"I wish to speak with Lord Aidan Weir," she said simply.

The guard did not blink. "The Garden of Flora favors anonymity, madam. Even if his lordship were within, I couldn't tell you."

What had she expected? A blissful welcome? That the guard spoke with the flawless elegance of the quality, however, was hardly surprising. Everything about the establishment had been carefully orchestrated to appeal to the upper echelons of society. Particularly its excesses. Voluptuaries flocked to The Garden of Flora in droves.

"If you will not tell me if he is within, then perhaps you will grant me entrance," she tried again.

She was determined to find Aidan.

"Unaccompanied ladies are not permitted within," the guard informed her.

She was aware of the rule, of course. On the previous occasions she had visited, she had always been with Aidan. She missed the scoundrel.

"I am a friend of Madame Laurent's," she said next, which was not entirely a falsehood. "Please tell her Miss Pen Sutton has come."

Well, perhaps mostly a falsehood. She had *met* The Garden of Flora's owner, a lovely and pleasant lady with a keen and cunning business acumen.

The guard's eyes narrowed. "A moment, miss."

The small door slid closed, and she was left to wait and wonder just how she would locate Aidan within if she were indeed granted entrance. Perhaps she had not thought her plan entirely through.

Before she had further time to contemplate the matter, the door opened fully to reveal a tall, all-too-familiar, form. He was dressed as elegantly as always. It was likely the miserable oaf never had so much as a hair out of place on his perfectly shaped head, nor a wrinkle in one of his immaculate cravats.

A scowl marred his otherwise handsome features. "Miss Sutton, what the devil are you doing here?" His voice was sharp, cutting through the air with the lash of a cracking whip.

He disapproved. But then, when had he not? From the moment he had first strode into her life, calling her a greedy fortune hunter and demanding she cry off her supposed betrothal to Aidan, Lord Lindsey had been looking down his aristocratic nose at her, finding her lacking. Judging her.

Even now, those icy-blue eyes told her everything she needed to know, burning into her with a searing intensity that stole her breath. For a heartbeat, she forgot what he had asked. She could do nothing more than stare at him stupidly, as if he were the first duke's heir she had ever seen.

In truth, she had seen many others of his ilk. Once, she had sung for their pleasure at The Sinner's Palace. Making them desire her had always held a surprising, almost fascinating source of power for Pen; earls and barons and marquesses wanting a lowly East End girl such as herself. But none of them could compare to the viscount. Never had she seen a man quite like this one, so impressive and foreboding without even trying.

She found her voice at last. "It is hardly any of your concern what I am doing here, my lord."

He continued to regard her with that imperious gaze, as if he had inspected her gown and found it covered in stains or marred by a torn hem. She barely suppressed the urge to look down and make certain her dress and pelisse were tidy enough.

"Come with me," he ordered crisply.

She eyed him warily. "I am not certain I ought to accompany you anywhere."

Thoughts of the passionate kisses they had shared, followed by his abrupt and cruel reaction to it, filled her mind.

His lip curled. "Now, Miss Sutton."

His determination to have her do his bidding heightened her own resolve to do the opposite. "I don't take my orders from you, Lord Lordly."

He moved forward, closing the distance between them, his expression grim. "You are the most infuriating female I have ever encountered."

Surely that was a compliment, coming from him.

Pen held her ground, refusing to retreat. "You are the most stubborn, arrogant, vexing…"

Her words faltered when he reached her and bent his tall form in half. No. There was absolutely no way he was going to do it. Her certainty faltered when his shoulder met her midriff. Surely he did not intend to…

He *did*.

He *was*.

The sheer audacity! Her shock and disbelief rendered her limp as a doll, all the lessons her brothers had taught her in defending herself against scoundrels falling into the dim cracks of her mind. Her opponent had been faster, the element of surprise aiding him.

Pen was being lifted through the air, as if she weighed no more than a farthing. The viscount had thrown her over his shoulder. His arms banded about her thighs, and then, he was moving, his long-limbed strides taking her only heaven knew where. The world was upside down. She was treated to a view of the elegant, thick woolen carpets of The Garden of Flora.

"Put me down," she commanded. "I've paid a hack to await me."

"I am sure the fellow will be more than amenable to keeping your coin and moving on," said the viscount grimly.

"My lord?" Another voice joined them, feminine and concerned. "This is most unusual, even by my standards."

"I require a chamber if you please, Sophie," he said, his voice a deep rumble that sent an elicit shiver through Pen even as her dudgeon over his overbearing actions remained high.

That unwanted reaction was swiftly chased by a nettlesome bolt of a different emotion. Apparently the rigidly proper viscount was familiar enough with Madame Laurent to call her by her given name.

"The rose room?" Madame asked, her unique, husky voice easily recognizable.

"Perfect," said the viscount, his ceaseless strides suggesting he was more than familiar with the landscape he currently inhabited.

The scoundrel.

The lessons her brothers had taught her returned. She curled her hands into fists and began beating on Lord Lordly's broad, infuriating back. "Let me down at once!"

"No," he said smoothly, before delivering a swat to her rump that rather stung.

Oh! Curse the devil! She was going to do far more than box his ears when she was on her feet. Her need to find Aidan had paled in comparison to her desire to inflict some vengeance upon his brother.

How dare he? He had no right to carry her about. To demand anything of her. He had asked her why she was here. She ought to have asked him the same question. What was *he* doing at The Garden of Flora?

No, she didn't want to know that, did she? The notion of him kissing one of the beautiful ladies added some muscle to her fists. She hit him harder, beating on his solid back to no avail. He delivered yet another sound spank to her bottom as she wriggled and fought, his strides never hesitating.

"Madame," she called, her desperation rising, "will you please aid me?"

But no one answered her, and she found herself being carried over a threshold, into a chamber with rose carpets. Red and white roses, everywhere. They swam beneath her as she bobbed on Lord Lordly's shoulder. A door snapped closed, indicating they were alone. She landed another few blows and was gratified at the grunting sound he emitted. She could only hope she had caused him some pain.

It would serve him right, the arsehole.

"That is quite enough, Miss Sutton," he said, bending to deposit her on the floor.

The moment she touched the floral carpets, she launched herself at him, intent upon doing him some manner of harm. He had been dogging her for days. Calling her everything but a lady. Insulting her with his bribery and his insistence she was nothing but a greedy, fortune-hunting manipulator who would marry any man as long as he was of the quality.

But he was quicker than she, blast him. He caught her wrist in a firm grip before she could plant him a proper facer, and his other arm snaked about her waist, hauling her tight to his body.

"Calm yourself, madam," he bit out, his tone harsh.

Well, he had only immobilized one fist, hadn't he?

Pen let the other one fly, taking him by surprise as she landed a blow on the sharp angle of his whisker-shadowed jaw. Pain shot from her knuckles, past her wrist, and all the way to her elbow. But she bit her lip to keep from crying out.

Lord Lordly had gone still. Pink blossomed on his jaw where her fist had connected with his flesh. "You will regret that," he said, part promise, part threat.

"Don't think I will," she countered, doing her utmost to keep her expression calm and controlled. "And there is more waiting for you if you run your rig any more than what you've already done."

She would not hesitate to punch him again, it was true. Although the red blooming on his otherwise flawless jaw did send a pinch of guilt lacing into her heart. She had never done another violence before. Leave it to Lord Lordly to be the first.

"I have no notion what you are speaking of, but if you dare to strike me again, you will suffer the consequences." His blue gaze was searing, his hold on her as rigid as his bearing.

He was all planes and sharp angles, Lord Lindsey, cutting as any blade, from his appearance to his voice to his words. Still, she would not be cowed by him. He was more powerful than she was, wealthier, taller, stronger, but she was a Sutton, by God. She was not afraid to stand up to anyone, his high and mighty lordship included.

"How?" she demanded, her defiance getting the better of her.

His nostrils flared. "Strike me again, and you shall see."

Even in his icy pique, he was strikingly handsome, and he had an effect upon her she could not like. Her insides were warm and melting and quivery, despite her outrage.

"You began this battle between us, as I recall," she pointed out.

And foolish, foolish, weak-willed Pen…her gaze dipped to his lips and her mouth tingled with the remembrance of his kisses.

His own lips parted, ever so slightly. For a moment, she wondered if he was plagued by similar thoughts.

But then he spoke again and rather ruined it.

"The only one responsible for the madness in which we find ourselves entangled is you, madam. If you had never attempted to ensnare my brother in matrimony, our paths would have failed to cross."

"Have you seen Aidan since you paid your last call upon me?" she asked, hoping that whilst her friend had clearly been ignoring her, he may have at least spoken with his overzealous brother and corrected some of his many assumptions about her.

"No," he said, spoiling those hopes.

"Neither have I," she admitted. "I was hoping to find him here tonight. He has ignored every note I have sent him since his announcement of our betrothal."

The despicable coward.

Perhaps she needed to rethink her choice of friends.

The viscount's gaze searched hers. "You came to find Aidan? What makes you believe he would be here?"

"Because he tends to think with his prick, much like every other man in London," she said crudely, hoping Lord Lordly would flinch, or at the very least go pale, at her inexcusable lack of manners.

But she was doomed to disappointment, for the viscount did nothing of the sort.

Instead, he continued to exhibit his signature, unflappable elegance, all flawless masculine perfection. "What a poor opinion you have of gentlemen, Miss Sutton."

"Perhaps it's because the lot of you do nothing but give me an aching head," she countered, feeling rather spiteful toward both Aidan and his insufferable brother. "And because none of you are truly gentleman. Not a one."

Briefly, she thought of one gentleman in particular and how easily charmed she had been. But then, she struck him from her mind.

"The sentiment is a mutual one," he told her. "From the moment my idiotic brother first spoke your name, I have been beset with nothing but problems. I dislike problems immensely, especially when they cannot be solved."

"I thought you already solved the problem of the mésalliance," she could not resist pointing out. "That was your intent in telling Aidan about kissing me, was it not? I imagine you sent him a note at once."

A hint of color shaded his angular cheekbones. "I have yet to inform him of your duplicity."

"Just *my* duplicity, Lord Lordly?" She raised a brow, vexed anew that he continued to pretend as if she had been alone in those passionate kisses.

As if he had been unaffected.

A certain portion of his anatomy most certainly had not been impervious at all.

His lip curled. "You are the one who betrayed your betrothed."

"And you are the one who betrayed his own brother by kissing his betrothed." Never mind that she and Aidan were not truly betrothed. The viscount didn't know that. Therefore, he was every bit as wrong and duplicitous as he supposed *she* was. Only more so, because she had no ties binding her to Aidan aside from his reckless declarations. "Need I remind you that your tongue was in my mouth and you were harder than—"

"Do not," he bit out, interrupting her, "say another word."

"Or what?" she dared to challenge him.

Or what indeed?

Miss Sutton was staring at him with such brazen defiance, awaiting his response, that for a moment, Garrick could not summon a reply. But the minx had been about to refer to the unfortunate effect kissing her had wreaked upon his cock. And that part of him had already come back to life the moment he had seen her standing on the other side of the private entrance to The Garden of Flora. He hardly required further incentive to want her, damn the fortune-hunting chit, despite all the reason and common sense he possessed.

He was painfully aware of her scent, her nearness, the specks of gold shimmering in her hazel eyes. Of those glorious lashes and all that stunning auburn hair which had formerly been shielded by her bonnet.

In the course of his carrying her to the rose room, the chapeau must have fallen somewhere to the floor. He wished it had not, for those lustrous locks gleamed in the light of the lamps, mocking him, calling for him to pull it free of hairpins and allow it to hang soft and heavy as a curtain down her back. His fingers itched to touch her. His mouth tingled with the memory of hers beneath it.

She had not been wrong to chastise him, even if it was not done for a woman in her position to take a stand against a man like him. He was every bit as guilty as she was, having kissed his brother's betrothed. And thus he remained, standing here in a bawdy house, lusting after her, longing to touch her again.

Knowing he must not.

Fingers aching with the need.

He tamped down a fresh swell of perverse desire.

"Enough," he managed curtly, speaking to himself as much as to her. "Cease your argument, madam. It is most unbecoming in a lady."

"But I'm not a lady, Lord Lordly," she said, her voice low and husky. Almost intimate. "And I don't give a damn if you consider my words unbecoming. I came here to find Aidan, and you're distracting me from my course. One can't help but to wonder why. Have you decided against telling him about our kiss for fear you'll incite your brother's wrath? Are you worried he will be outraged to know your mouth was on his future wife's? That you kissed me as if you wanted me in your bed beneath you?"

Curse the jade.

Her words had what was no doubt their intended effect, producing not just a tide of anger rising to the surface, but a hailstorm of need as well. His reaction was as despicable as it was instant. He could not seem to keep himself from thinking about her in his bed. Beneath him, just as she had taunted. Her soft, lush curves melting against his body, thighs parting for him to settle between, thrusting his cock deep into the inviting heat of her cunny as she arched her back and moaned his name.

My God, man. What have you become?

He loathed himself.

But his cock was suddenly thick and hard, pressing against the fall of his trousers. An attraction to the forbidden was nothing new to Garrick, but how unfair it was to be a servant to the whim of his own desires with this woman in particular, of all the fairer sex. She could not be more wrong—beneath him in class, manners, betrothed to his brother, a cunning fortune-hunter all too eager for a title. Far too similar to Veronica.

Unfortunately, he could not seem to relay that missive to his prick.

He forced a confident, cool smile. It was one he used often and which served him well whenever he wished to remind those present that he was the heir to the Duke of Dryden, and that he was one of the most powerful arbiters of polite society.

Against his better judgment, Garrick leaned toward her. "Take care, my greedy little fortune hunter. It sounds to me as if you are speaking of your own feverish longings rather than mine. Never fear, madam. Do not think yourself the first. I am well accustomed to women who set their caps at me."

It was true. Half the chits in London swooned if he so much as gazed in their direction across a ballroom. All the bucks wanted to be him. The ladies wanted to marry him. The widows and the unsatisfied wives wanted him in their bedchambers.

Her gaze narrowed. "The only thing I would like to set at you is my fist. I've already done so once. Don't think I'll not give you another poke. A nice, sound basting is what you need, my lord. Bring a scant hint of sense into that knowledge box of yours."

Something snapped inside him.

Patience, sanity, outrage? He could not say. The string had rent, whatever it was, and the twain ends would never again meet. A shift happened. And then his hands were moving. Reaching for her. Finding the deliciously feminine curves of her waist beneath her pelisse and gown, pulling her nearer.

She came willingly, her hands on his chest, soft and hesitant as butterflies. There was no rejection, no effort made to push him away or escape. His head dipped, mouth seeking hers as if it were the most natural act, as if it were inevitable.

And inevitable it was.

His senses were aflame. The touch of her lips to his

ignited a conflagration. God, her mouth felt good. Silken and hot and delicious. Why? Why should this woman, above any other, affect him thus? Her lips opened, and he forgot to care. He cupped her face, angling her head so he could deepen the kiss, and licked into her mouth. The delicate whimper of surrender that left her was enough to make him almost dizzied with lust. Their tongues moved together, and he could not suppress his groan of raw need.

He was so damned hard, the fit of his trousers making his cockstand almost painful. But he liked it. He liked the way she made him feel. Desperate and greedy and sinful and powerful all at once. He would give in for this moment. Perhaps another.

His fingers were moving of their own accord, finding those hated hairpins that were keeping her locks in such a careful, plain chignon and plucking them away. *Ping, ping, ping.* They rained upon the rose carpets.

Roses, yes.

Reality intruded. He was at The Garden of Flora where each private chamber possessed a floral theme. Sophie was circumspect; she would guard a man's secret with her life, for her trustworthiness was her livelihood. The rest of the staff as well knew to keep the habits of their patrons quiet. Still, he could not afford to ruin himself here in such fashion. He needed to remember the reason he had come to begin with.

Two reasons, in truth.

The first had been to determine if his brother was present. The second had been to distract himself from the very persistent, wholly unwanted longings which had been plaguing him for days.

The longings that kept him from stopping now.

Just a moment more.

Another kiss.

Their mouths moved in feverish unison, teeth nipping,

tongues tangling. It was raw and furious, anger mixed with undiluted lust. And he had never experienced anything quite so exquisite.

He wanted to consume her, to mark her, to bring her to her knees, to conquer and claim her. And then he wanted her to conquer and claim him in return. This passionate creature would never be happy as his brother's wife. She would make Aidan's life a misery.

Perhaps Garrick ought to take a mistress after all.

No! What was wrong with him? He was stronger than his desires.

He tore his mouth from Miss Sutton's and straightened to his full height, irritated at the raggedness of his breathing, the erratic beats of his heart, the longing still filling him with desire.

They stood there together, hands still on each other's bodies, gazes locked.

"Aidan isn't here, Miss Sutton," he forced himself to say.

He ought to have told her before, it was true. But he had been initially so nettled at her appearance, and then determined to discover if she knew more about where Aidan could have gone, and then just as hastily, he had been desperate to kiss her. To own her mouth with his.

The things he could show her. *Lord God.*

But then, who knew how innocent she was. Likely, there were quite a few skills *she* might show him.

Unworthy thoughts, borne of the sinner within.

"You know he is not here for certain?" Miss Sutton asked, her full, well-kissed lips compressing into a pout.

"I do."

The shove to his chest took him by surprise. Fortunately, he was naturally graceful, and he caught his balance rather than toppling backward on his arse.

"You could have said as much rather than carting me over your shoulder," she said, her voice sharp.

He winced, for once again, she was not wrong. "I wished to speak with you in a private setting, and you were being stubbornly vexing."

"Hmm," was all she said, raising a brow and regarding him in such a manner that suggested she did not believe him.

Not for a moment.

And well, curse her again.

"Where is Aidan, if he is not here?" she asked then.

Aidan.

Of course she was concerned with the man she intended to dupe into marriage. His ardor cooled at the reminder. "I haven't an inkling where he is hiding himself."

"Did you come here to find him as well?"

"Why else should I be present at such an establishment?" he returned, careful to keep his tone mild lest she suspect him of having ventured here to sate his carnal appetites.

Not that it mattered what she thought. She was a mere East End nobody.

One you cannot stop kissing or lusting after.

Blast!

Miss Sutton's hazel gaze was studying him in a way he could not like. Seeing him, he thought. Seeing far too much of him.

"I'm sure I couldn't say why you might be visiting a nunnery, Lord Lordly," she said, her voice taunting.

He could not get out of this woman's presence soon enough. What madness had overtaken him where she was concerned?

"Since we have both quenched our curiosity concerning my brother's whereabouts, we shouldn't tarry in Madame Laurent's chamber." He kept his voice cold and his countenance—he hoped—every bit as frigid.

"At last, we have found a subject upon which we can agree, my lord. I bid you good evening."

She dipped into a small, angry curtsy while he offered her an aggravated bow.

And as quickly as she had appeared to upset his evening, Miss Sutton turned her back on him and left.

CHAPTER 5

Filial guilt was little different than a boulder hanging from one's damned neck. That was why Garrick had agreed to escort Mother to the Rivendale Assembly Rooms this evening instead of paying a call to The Garden of Flora as he so desperately wished. The gathered revelers before them, swirling about in a lively Scotch reel, held no interest to him.

Nor did the overly tart lemonade, buttered bread, or dry cakes being offered in the supper rooms.

Although he was carrying on as if nothing had altered, politely conversing with anyone he deemed worthy of his attention, dutifully fetching Mother fresh lemonade when she complained the crush was rendering her uncomfortably warm, and otherwise behaving like the dutiful son he was, everything had changed. It did not matter that Lady Hester was in attendance, or that she was dressed in a becoming gown that perfectly complemented her golden hair. It did not matter that he had once found the dances at Rivendale's an utterly enthralling use of his evening.

Because thoughts of one woman were plaguing him with galling persistence.

"I am considering allowing Lady Fern Grant a voucher," Mother was saying. "What do you think, Lindsey?"

Mother was one of the original patronesses of Rivendale's, a rival establishment of Almack's, which she had sponsored after an argument with one of the imperious patronesses of that peculiar institution some years ago. In true Mother fashion, she had worked tirelessly to turn Rivendale's into the shining gem of polite society it now was. They were more exclusive than Almack's, their vouchers more costly and sought-after.

Miss Penelope Sutton would never be accepted within these walls, it was certain. But why should the thought occur to him at all? And worse, why should it be accompanied by a pang of regret? There was a reason society had rules, after all, and it was to keep women of her ilk where they belonged.

"Lindsey?"

Mother's indignant tone reminded him he had yet to offer his opinion on the matter she had presented.

He suppressed a sigh of irritation. "Yes, do allow Lady Felicity Vere a voucher."

"You were not listening, were you?" his mother demanded, her frown as fierce as her displeasure. "I was speaking of Lady Fern, not Lady Felicity."

The wrong Lady F. And all because he had been too busy thinking about a woman who was not a lady at all. A woman he never should have touched or kissed. A woman who most certainly ought not to be haunting his every waking—and sleeping—hour. A woman who was his brother's betrothed.

For now, he reminded himself. As soon as he found Aidan, that would change. He simply had to find the devil. Garrick appreciated the irony that his always predictable, ever-reckless brother appeared to have suddenly become irregularly, unusually, and impossibly circumspect ever since his fateful announcement concerning his unacceptable betrothal.

Naturally, this was the manner in which the world worked. Or perhaps merely the manner in which Aidan worked.

"Forgive me," he told his mother, tamping down his irritation, "I was distracted."

"By Lady Hester, no doubt," his mother said with a raised brow. "She is lovely. You have chosen well, my darling."

He followed her gaze to where his future wife was executing a flawless reel. Her every movement was sheer elegance; she moved with the practiced grace of a lady who had been carefully and properly schooled in the art of dance. Naturally so. She was the daughter of an incredibly wealthy, well-connected, and highly respected earl. Garrick watched her effortless motions and wished he felt a stirring of…something.

Anything.

But there was nothing within. Not a hint of interest, nary a twitch of awareness. He was not singularly aflame as he was whenever Miss Sutton was within proximity. No indeed, Lady Hester was not his source of distraction. But he would never admit otherwise. He could concede his abject failure to himself alone. It was just as well, for no one else judged Garrick as harshly as he did himself.

"Thank you, Mother," he offered distractedly, searching the room for a suitable excuse for escape. The glare of the chandeliers overhead was suddenly stifling, his cravat felt as if it were a noose, and he was incredibly aggrieved with himself. The latter, of course, was nothing new. "I am confident Lady Hester will make an excellent viscountess."

"And one day duchess."

His mother's softly spoken words were an unwanted reminder of the tentative health of his father. The duke was weak, it was true. This terrible business with Aidan—first announcing his intention to wed a thoroughly unsuitable bride and then disappearing—could well prove more than his heart was able to bear.

A chill chased down Garrick's spine, his gut clenching.

No. Father was far too important, far too powerful a man, to go to his eternal reward with such haste. Now was not the time. All Garrick needed to do was find his brother and set this infernal tangle to rights. It could be done, he was sure of it.

It *had* to be done.

The ramifications, not just for Father, but for Mother as well, were far too dire.

"I prefer not to contemplate that unwanted day," he told his mother, swallowing a lump of emotion that had risen in his throat.

"It is the natural order of our lives," Mother said calmly, as if she were not speaking of the death of her husband, Garrick's father. "None of us shall live forever, and that is why deciding upon a future husband or wife carries such unfathomable importance. You are a credit to the line, my lord."

A credit to the line.

Always, forever, *the line*. The duchy, the Weir family name and reputation, their position in society. Why had he never tired of the endless worries before now?

Garrick summoned a smile he did not feel. "It is my duty."

And it was. Marrying the right woman, begetting an heir and a spare, making certain there would be nary a whisper of scandal and impropriety about his name or that of his future wife's...these were all the heavy weights which rested upon Garrick's shoulders. He was the future Duke of Dryden, and he had been reminded of that salient fact from the moment he had been old enough to speak his own cursed name.

Oddly, the yoke had never felt so heavy a burden as it did now. Was Lady Hester truly what he wanted in a wife? A woman he had never been motivated to kiss? Perhaps he ought to at least try before shackling himself to her forever.

"At least two of my sons understand what is expected of them," Mother said then, making a small huff of dissatisfaction to punctuate her words. "Your youngest brother…I do despair, though I dare not speak of *the unfortunate situation* in public."

Aidan again. Blast him, always the source of trouble and discord. And blast Miss Sutton, for never straying far from Garrick's thoughts or conversations. It seemed that every discussion he entered with his parents referenced her, and she most certainly haunted his thoughts.

"A wise decision not to speak of it," he agreed, for even the potted plants at Rivendale's seemed to possess acutely listening ears and correspondingly wagging tongues.

Damn it, he needed to find his brother and put an end to this business with Miss Sutton. Surely it was the incomplete nature of the matter, far more than anything else, which had him feeling distinctly on edge this evening. Rendering him incapable of fully enjoying the social event as he ought.

Surely someone in attendance was a friend of Aidan's.

They should know where he was hiding himself. Where he had gone. Why.

Garrick cast his gaze about the ballroom, desperately seeking and searching. At last, he spied one of his brother's ne'er-do-well friends. Relief washed over him, nearly palpable. "Ah, forgive me for the distraction, but I do see Lord Carstairs just across the ballroom. I fear that I must speak with him about a pressing matter of great concern. If you will excuse me, Mother dearest?"

A pressing matter of great concern was the phrase Garrick always relied upon whenever he wished to excuse himself from his mother's presence. He had learned it from his father, and he had no doubt Father had been taught the same unique means of escape from an unwanted discussion by Grandfather, and so on, delving back into the annals of family history to the times of William the Conqueror. The women of the Weir family had been carefully selected, born and bred to understand that the complexities of their husbands' lives were none of their concern.

Lady Hester was no different. She would never question him, raise her voice, or offer opposition. This, Garrick knew. She would never dare to give him a poke in the jaw, as Miss Sutton had done. She would not look upon him with fury or kiss him with passion. Her mouth would not make him desperate to claim it. And he would never be filled with the fiery, all-consuming need to have her in his bed.

But that was the natural, proper order of life in the *ton*. Marriages were made for practical reasons. Money, *éclat*, expectations of one's parents, unions between families, property, society.

"Of course, my lord." Mother smiled. "I shall see you later, before you retire to your club, shan't I?"

He often remained at these events for hours, with the sole purpose of keeping Mother content. There were ordinarily any number of acquaintances with whom he might fight his *ennui*. The right word here, the proper connection there, and a man's power and influence could steadily grow. Garrick's certainly had. However, he found his patience and his desire to observe the social whirl steadily waning this evening.

Quite unusually so.

"I shall try," he told Mother rather than promising.

It was the best he could offer.

This evening's entertainments left him feeling strangely bereft and hollow and…*itchy*. Was it the absence of his brother or the unexpected effects of Miss Sutton in his life which had caused the sea change? Garrick could not say for certain.

All he knew was that something had to be done.

And with bloody haste.

He could not find Aidan soon enough. For finding him meant removing Miss Sutton from his own life.

Forever.

THERE WERE ONLY SO many blasted places Lord Aidan Weir could hide.

But Pen was reasonably certain she had already searched them all.

Still, he could not have simply vanished from London. He would not have left, not without leaving some word for her. The more days that passed without him patronizing The Sinner's Palace or at least sending her a note, the more worried she became.

Where could he have gone?

Pen was determined to find out.

Which was why she had bound her breasts and was dressed in the trousers and coat she had donned whenever she and Aidan attended bare-knuckle boxing matches together. It was also why she had greased the palm of a lad at the trade entrance of the club on St. James's Street that Aidan favored.

The Duke's Bastard was where nobs gathered to drink and eat and gamble when they had no wish to sully themselves with the riffraff of the East End. Duncan Kirkwood, the owner of the club, was the illegitimate son of a duke and had built an empire for himself that had not gone unnoticed by Pen's oldest brother Jasper. After the building they had intended to use as The Sinner's Palace II had been burned down, Jasper had suggested they set their caps at the West End instead. And so they had.

We could bring a rival to The Duke's Bastard, Jasper had said.

But as Pen slipped through its hallowed halls, she knew they would have quite a bit of work ahead of them to provide a proper rival. The Duke's Bastard had become one of the most exclusive clubs for the quality, and she understood the reason why. Rich, sleek woods enhanced the paneled walls, which were adorned by paintings and gilt-and-mirrored wall sconces. It appeared as if Mr. Kirkwood had spared no expense.

The Duke's Bastard was decidedly not the sort of establishment where a Sutton would be welcomed at the door—everything about it, from the murals gracing the walls as she reached the public halls, to the rich carpets, suggested it had been created for the quality alone. Most particularly, a *female* Sutton would never be invited within. Hence the necessity for discretion. And since she was a Sutton, such an objective had only been achieved by bribery and dressing as a cove.

She knew nary a hint of guilt as she found her way through the maze of halls, ducking shadows and footsteps at every turn. Raised masculine voices around a corner had her slipping into an alcove and holding her breath until the men inevitably traveled in the opposite direction. Having reached her majority living within a gaming hell, Pen had no trouble finding her way. One could locate the kitchen by its scent—rich foods being expertly crafted by Kirkwood's famous French chef, no doubt—and the rumble of more voices told her where the gaming rooms could be found.

At last, Pen stood in one of the main public halls, and judging from the gentlemen moving about at the opposite end, it was likely the hall where the necessary house was located. East End or West End, some things never changed. The more a man drank, the more he had to piss.

How convenient. Finding an area where gentlemen were coming and going would prove an excellent foil for her ruse. Pen hastened her strides lest the lad she had paid decided his loyalty was to his employer instead. She was moving so quickly, determined to find her way into the game rooms and discover whether or not Aidan was within, that she did not see the man exiting a door until he was before her, and she had plowed directly into his broad chest.

The chest was familiar.

"You again."

So, too, the deep, disapproving growl.

Biting her lip, Pen glanced up into the handsome face of the man who had so swiftly become her archenemy. Her heart dropped to the soles of the boots Aidan had given her to wear on their clandestine outings.

Lord Lordly. Blast the man. Why was he always everywhere she was? Pen had a moment to decide how she would allow this scene to play out.

Lowering her head and using the brim of her hat to shield her face, she cleared her throat and endeavored to speak in her most manly voice. "Forgive me," she said, stepping to her left and attempting to skirt around him.

Perhaps he would think he had mistaken her for someone else. Her voice sounded quite masculine when she made a concerted effort to render it low and rough. Did it not?

A finger caught in the collar of her coat, staying her forward motion.

Perhaps not.

"What the devil do you think you are doing?" he demanded, apparently not fooled at all.

Would the blasted cove never cease plaguing her?

"Seeking distraction," she ground out, "just as all my fellow gentlemen in attendance this evening are."

Somehow, perpetuating her lie seemed important, if for

no other reason than to nettle the man at her back. Surrendering would be akin to admitting defeat, and she would not leave The Duke's Bastard until she could be certain Aidan was not within its walls.

"Making more trouble for me," countered the viscount, "*that* is what you are truly doing. Come with me, Miss Sutton."

Her name was a hushed hiss, letting her know that he saw through her disguise and that he did not wish to draw attention to them. She watched with frustration and disappointment as a gentleman who appeared on the cusp of maudlin drunk swayed as he made his way back to the main gaming rooms down the hall.

She tore away from the viscount's grasp and spun to face him. The light from the sconces caught on his slashing cheekbones, brilliant eyes, and sculpted lips. It seemed vastly unfair for the Lord to have made a man so beautifully handsome and yet such an arrogant arsehole, all at once. But then, that was the way of things, wasn't it?

"I won't go anywhere with you," she said, her stubbornness rising. She was a Sutton, and Suttons did not do what they were told. "I have some matters to attend to in the gaming room."

The smile he flashed her was grim and made her traitorous heart trip over itself as an accompanying flash of heat bolted through her. "I am afraid you misunderstand, my dear. I did not give you the option of denying me."

The arrogance of the man would have astounded her had she not already experienced it on every occasion their paths had thus far crossed. "I'm not your dear, you oaf."

The patronizing manner in which he employed the endearment made her long to poke him in his lordly jaw again. But now was neither the time nor the place.

His lips compressed into a forbidding frown, and she

could not help but to recall what that mouth felt like on hers, kissing her so expertly. "I have no wish to be caught with you in this establishment, madam. I have managed to live two-and-thirty years without the taint of scandal, and I will not allow you to dash my reputation to bits."

His cold scorn vexed her mightily.

She planted her hands on her hips. "Then please do go elsewhere, Lord Lordly. I have no need for your presence."

His nostrils flared. "I cannot go elsewhere when I know you are gadding about dressed as a gentleman."

He truly was the most ridiculous man. "Why not?"

"My honor will not allow it," he said through clenched teeth.

Pen almost laughed, but he was serious, his countenance chillier than winter and every bit as frozen. "You can save your breath to cool your porridge, my lord. I'll be moving along."

Of course, Lord Lordly likely did not eat anything as common as porridge. But never mind. He could take his honor and shove it up his arse. She turned on her heel.

"Damn it, you troublesome minx."

His muttered words were her only warning. In the next instant, a strong arm banded around her waist, hauling her backward, over a threshold and into a chamber. The door closed. Pen had a brief impression of lewd murals and more glittering, mirrored wall sconces before the instinct to remove herself from Lord Lordly's overbearing clutches returned.

She attempted to wrest herself free, but he was as strong as those broad shoulders and thick arms beneath his coat suggested. She could not free herself regardless of how much she struggled.

He spun them about suddenly, pressing her back to the door and pinning her in place with his body. His palms flattened to the door on either side of her head. His knee slipped between her legs, unimpeded by the gowns and petticoats she would have ordinarily worn.

"What the devil do you think you're about?" she asked as she squirmed, still determined to flee him.

"Stop moving," he ground out, his jaw clenched.

Naturally, she ignored him, continuing to wriggle, her palms flattened on his chest. His heat seared her through her gloves, the rippling of his muscles as he worked to subdue her strangely pleasant. Her actions made his thigh settle at the apex of hers, wedging there.

And the connection between their bodies sent a jolt from her core that rushed through the rest of her.

Heavens. She was not meant to enjoy this. Venturing within The Duke's Bastard this evening had not been so that she would again cross verbal swords with the viscount, but rather so she might see for herself whether or not Aidan was within. And yet, what a terrible friend she was proving to be.

For she was not thinking of Aidan at all in this moment.

How could she?

The viscount was holding her to the door, dressed as if he had been gracing a ducal ballroom this evening, perfect and handsome and infuriating and everything she should not want. Everything that was forbidden to her. Her friend's lordly older brother. A man who believed her to be nothing more than a fortune hunter who was attempting to wed Aidan so she could amuse herself with drawing room visits and trips to the *modiste.*

But her desire was burning hotter than the fires of Hades itself.

His lordship's breathing was harsh. For a few heartbeats, they remained as they were, utterly still, bodies pressed together. His scent wrapped around her like a lover's embrace. And then he shifted. Subtly. Scarcely any movement at all, but she noticed it. Oh, how she noticed it. His leg slid more firmly between hers, pressing deliciously into her awakened flesh.

Her lips parted. The fight fled her. When his gaze dipped to her mouth, she was ready and willing, already anticipating his kiss. But he was not as hasty as she would have liked. Instead, he allowed his gaze to linger, as tempting as a touch, and swallowed hard. She watched the maddening dip of his Adam's apple above his expertly knotted cravat.

"This is your fault, Miss Sutton," he said crisply.

Coolly.

As politely as she imagined he would if they were facing each other in a society drawing room.

And then he quite made a lie of that frigid display of well-mannered gallantry by lowering his mouth to hers.

Sweet angels and saints.

The urge to fight him was gone. In its place was that same welcoming surrender she seemed to experience whenever he was near enough, his dangerous proximity rendering her weak. Inexplicable, thoroughly unwanted, and yet nonetheless true. Her arms wound around his neck, holding him close. His lips slanted over hers in a kiss that was almost harsh in its insistence. Firm and demanding, his warm mouth caressed hers with such stunning hunger that she was helpless to do anything but respond.

The viscount could kiss, blast his arrogant hide.

His tongue dipped inside her mouth, and he tasted of tart citrus.

He had been consuming lemonade, she thought, which seemed decidedly at odds with a gentleman who was at his club. He ought to taste of brandy or some other such spirit. But then, if she had learned anything from her brief acquaintance with Lord Lindsey, it was that he was a man of surprising disparities.

He was calm and gentlemanly, polished and perfect in true nob fashion. And then, by turns, wild. As he was now, trapping her to the door and devouring her with his mouth. He played the part of gallant viscount well, but he did not fool her. He was no stranger to iniquity.

His lips traveled along her jaw, stringing a path of unquenchable yearning in their wake. When he found her ear, he kissed the shell, his breath making a shiver of desire roll down her spine. Her nipples, already painfully pressed within the binding she had donned for this excursion, ached.

She knew from experience just how delightful a touch could be on them. But no one before the viscount had ever made her feel such shattering desire. Her entire body, from the soles of her feet, to the very roots of her hair, felt astonishingly alive.

Alive, and desperate for more.

His lips grazed the whorls of flesh she had not even known would crave such attention until now. Her knees threatened to give out. The abrasion of her undergarments beneath the too-large male trousers, coupled with the pressure of his thigh, sent pulsating awareness blossoming from her cunny.

That sinful tongue flicked over her flesh, and then his teeth caught the upper curve of her ear, biting. Marking her, it seemed. Claiming in an elemental fashion.

"You are a wretched annoyance, Miss Sutton," he murmured into her ear.

But while his words were unkind, his tone was nothing short of deep, dark seduction. Velvet and silk to her senses.

She rubbed her cheek against his, relishing the prickle of his whiskers on her sensitive skin. "As are you, my lord."

"I should fuck you right here, right now." He dragged his lips lower, down her throat to where her pulse pounded just above her cravat. "That is what you want, is it not?"

His unexpected crudity shocked her. Not because she had never heard such vulgar language before. She was a Sutton who had been born and raised in the rookeries. She had heard and seen all. But because from him, it was unprecedented. And far from being a loss of control, there was something about his words and his actions that seemed alarmingly deliberate in a bold new way.

Accompanying the shock permeating her lust-addled mind was another question. What would it be like to take this man as her lover?

He sucked on her neck, then gently bit the tender cord there. "Answer me."

Did she want him to bed her? Her body most certainly did. Her pride, however, would allow no such admission.

"You are astoundingly sure of yourself," she managed, irritated with herself at the breathlessness in her voice.

So much for seeming unaffected.

"Your body tells me everything I need to know." His right hand moved from the door to slip beneath her coat and caress her waist first, then her hip. "If I reach into your trousers right now, I am willing to wager I would find your cunny dripping for me."

No one had ever spoken to her thus, and the effect was potent. She almost begged him to do it and put the both of them out of their misery. But then she remembered that this was Aidan's brother and he thought incredibly poorly of her, and that if she were to allow him such liberties, he would likely only crow about it later.

His fingers trailed a tantalizing path over her trousers, gliding nearer to where she ached. Up her inner thigh. She should tell him to stop. Shove him away instead of holding him close. She did not feel at all threatened by the viscount, and nor did she believe he would press his suit if she were to deny him. And the truth of it was, she did not truly want him to cease his seduction.

She wanted him to continue.

He skimmed his fingers along the seam at the juncture of her thighs with tantalizing slowness. Nothing more than the lightest of pressure, a butterfly's wings.

Not enough.

She jerked into his touch, riding his thigh. He stilled, his head lifting with agonizing torpor. There was surprise in his countenance. Perhaps she had shocked him with her response. Heavens, she had stunned herself. His gaze met hers, searching, seeking.

Part of her wanted to look away, sever the connection, and yet she could not. In the flickering candlelight, the icy-blue of his eyes took on a deeper hue, akin to the sky after midnight.

"Shall I touch you, then?" he asked, his voice thick with desire.

He wanted her.

That was understood, for she had felt his body's reaction to hers before when he had been so intimately pressed against her. But she had supposed his previous reaction had been natural, caused by the fact that she was a woman and he had kissed her. This, however, what was suddenly unfolding between them, bore the distinct hallmark of something altogether different. Indeed, he did not just want her. He was wooing her.

He was taking his time. Seducing her with bold words and knowing caresses. Teasing her. Bringing her to the edge so that she was forced to either admit she wanted him too or retreat in thwarted desire. Was it his conceit that made him so bold?

His thumb brushed over the fall of her trousers, unerringly strumming directly above the place where the seat of her pleasure dwelled. He grazed her bud. How she longed to know his bare flesh on hers, rather than through the barrier of layers of fabric.

Still not sufficient.

These teasing, taunting passes of his thumb were intentional, she knew. He watched her silently, his stare growing hooded.

"Yes," she said at last, the word a reluctant hiss.

She had not come to The Duke's Bastard seeking Viscount Lindsey. Indeed, she had been doing her utmost to forget about his very existence and to carry on as if she had never met him. His insults had faded to the back of her mind. She had been singularly devoting herself, instead, to finding her friend so that she might box his ears and then direct him to inform his family he had been deceiving them when he had announced their betrothal.

But all her intentions and motivations, even her pride, fell away when the viscount's long, elegant fingers—fingers she had admired on previous occasions most unwillingly—found the fastening on the fall of her trousers. A few swift movements, his eyes searing into hers all the while, and the flap dropped.

A wisp of cool air invaded, teasing her. Holding her gaze, he replaced the air with his fingers. He stroked her tentatively, tenderly, tracing her seam to the pulsating bud hidden within her folds. His forefinger moved with expert attention, sending pleasure radiating from her core.

Her body had a life and mind of its own, hips bucking, heart pounding, her hold on his neck tightening.

"Just as I thought," he said, his low voice sending an answering spark of awareness to join the others he had already started. "You are wet. So wet."

She was. How shameful, and yet, she could not summon the urge to care in this moment of defiant, soul-destroying desire. His fingers were gliding over her, aided by the natural dew her body had produced. The sign she wanted him despite his arrogance and his highhanded behavior.

"Do you want to be fucked here and now, against this door?" he asked, finding an especially sensitive place and tormenting her with a combination of swirling pressure that had her nearly dizzied with need.

She ought to tell him *no*. To deny him. To deny them both. This was the very sort of dalliance her brothers continually warned her against. It was the reason they had all disapproved of her friendship with Aidan. They had been convinced he wanted to bed her rather than befriend her, and that he would leave her with a bastard and without a backward glance.

From the time she had been old enough to understand the differences between men and women, her siblings had warned her that wealthy nobs like their patrons would never marry a lowly Sutton girl. They had taught her that powerful men were quick to take advantage of powerless women and use them for their pleasures before discarding them for the next victim who believed she may somehow secure a protector or perhaps even a husband.

But she would not.

Just as Lord Lordly would never marry Pen. She doubted he would even lower himself enough to ask her to be his mistress. But that was fine. She was not setting her cap for either role.

"Say something, damn you," he growled.

It was his loss of polish and wintry condescension that sent Pen spiraling over the cliffs of Thou Shalt Not. She tumbled arsy-varsy to the jagged rocks below.

"Yes," she said, forgetting all the reasons why she must never agree to anything with this man.

Forgetting everything but his body burning into hers, his knowing touch, the fires of need he had stoked so expertly.

A knock sounded on the door.

"Anyone within?" asked a masculine voice from the other side.

Pen's heart froze.

The viscount stilled. "Yes," he called out, his voice carrying the stinging remonstration of a cat-o'-nine-tails. "Very much so."

"Beg pardon," grumbled the other voice.

Footsteps sounded in the hall, moving away.

Lord Lindsey withdrew from her with such haste, Pen nearly fell to the floor.

"Christ." He scrubbed a hand over his face. "What the hell was I thinking?"

Pen did not bother to say she knew the answer to his query. For it was quite plain he had not been thinking. Nor had she.

Her fingers, still gloved, flew to the fall of her trousers, attempting to rectify the damage he had done. But curse it, buttons were nearly impossible to secure in their moorings in such a state.

What a dreadful, terrible coil.

He raked a hand through his hair, watching her struggle, before stepping toward her again.

"Allow me." He brushed her fingers aside and nimbly fastened the fall.

She supposed he ought to be well-practiced at the art of fastening a gentleman's rigging. He was one, after all.

Pen tamped down the rising tide of embarrassment threatening to crash over her head. It would not do to allow this man to see her weakness. Knowing him, he would only find some means of using it to his advantage.

"Thank you," she said briskly, moving away from the door on the shaky legs of a newborn foal.

What had he done to her?

Moreover, why had she allowed it?

Worse still, why had she wanted it, wanted *him,* and so desperately?

"We are not finished, Miss Sutton," the viscount said, a hint of warning in his tone.

She inhaled slowly, trying to calm herself and regain her inner sense of calm. She felt as if she had been aboard a storm-tossed vessel for weeks, and now she had been suddenly delivered to a cloudless shore, expected to forget everything which had come to pass before.

"We are indeed finished, Lord Lordly, if we had ever begun," she managed, careful to keep her voice cool.

She had no wish for him to understand just how deeply he had affected her. Or just how badly she desired him, how her heart was racing faster than the hooves of a galloping stallion, how her body still hungered for his touch and her lips thrummed with the memory of his upon them.

"You are wrong, madam." He spoke just as coolly, his countenance implacable, as if he had not just been speaking to her with such delicious lewdness, touching her as if it were his right, kissing her as if he would die if he did not have another taste of her lips. "We are quite far from finished. But this is hardly the time or the place for what must come to pass. How did you find your way in here?"

The knowledge felt quite dear. If he wanted it, she would withhold the information.

"I walked," she said, not bothering to hide her insolence.

The walls between them had crumbled some time ago, and there was nary a chance of them being erected again. He may well be the heir to a duke, and he could look down his aristocratic nose at her all he liked, but he desired her as a woman, and that knowledge in itself was every bit as powerful as his position in London society, for she could use it to her advantage quite well.

He clenched his jaw. "Naturally. I had supposed you may have sprouted wings and flown, but I must express my most humble gratitude to you for disabusing me of my false suppositions."

He certainly spoke in riddles and rhymes, but he was plainly attempting to offer her a sally. The gesture was so unexpected that she hesitated in her response.

A bit too long.

His hand clamped on her elbow. Not in a bruising grip, but in one that told her he would not release her without a fight. And after what had just happened between them, waging war was hardly likely. At least on her behalf. One could scarcely tell what was happening behind those eerie blue eyes of Lord Lordly's.

"I hardly think we can leave this establishment with you clinging to my elbow," she pointed out wryly. "The tongues you have no wish to give cause for wagging will be racing instead."

"There is more than one entrance to The Duke's Bastard," he said, his gaze flicking over her face in a seeking fashion, "as you are undoubtedly aware. We shall take our withdrawal through one of those."

How like a member of the quality to suppose the men and women circulating in the service quarters would be too busy toiling at their various positions to take note of a lord hauling another gentleman from the club by his elbow.

"Once again, your utter arrogance astounds, Lord Lordly," she drawled, taking a small amount of pleasure from the manner in which he flinched at her use of the insulting title she had fashioned just for him.

Just as well.

Who did he think he was, kissing her as he had? Saying such wicked things to her, unbuttoning the fall of her trousers, insinuating his well-muscled thigh between her legs?

"It is confidence, Miss Sutton," he corrected, raising a dark brow, "not arrogance. The difference is easily distinguished, should one concern one's self with looking."

She pursed her lips. "Naturally, I do not tax myself where you are concerned. Why should it matter?"

He inclined his head. "Why indeed? Nonetheless, I insist you accompany me. There is much that needs to be discussed between the two of us."

She frowned. "I find no such need."

Lord Lordly smiled, showing neat, even teeth.

He had the smile and charm of a sinner and the reputation of a saint. Which one was he, she wondered? But then, the answer was abundantly obvious, was it not?

"Come with me, Miss Sutton, and I shall elaborate."

It was not truly an invitation. Rather, it was a warning laced with the pretensions of an arrogant lord and the suggestion he knew more of Aidan's whereabouts than he had initially suggested.

Her interest was piqued. "Very well, Lord Lordly," she allowed. "I will accompany you. But it'll be on my terms, not yours."

She did not wait for him to have the last word before she gave him her back and left the chamber.

CHAPTER 6

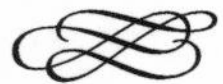

The house where he had kept his former mistress had been empty for several months in anticipation of his impending betrothal. There was absolutely no reason why Garrick should, at this very moment, be escorting his brother's unsuitable betrothed over its threshold whilst she was dressed in the shabbiest guise of a gentleman he had ever beheld.

None save lunacy.

And that was most definitely his motivator. It *had* to be. How else could he explain bringing her here, where they would be utterly alone and where he knew there was a most accommodating bed?

"Surely you did not expect to fool anyone with this ludicrous garb," he could not resist commenting as he lit a candelabra within the front entry, sending light to illuminate her clearly feminine form.

Any man would have to take but one look at her to note her hips and arse, her lovely face and skin as soft as silk. There was nothing masculine about her. True, she had obviously gone to some lengths to flatten her generous breasts. He hated to think of the torture she must have subjected them to, and the worst part of him thought about how he would like to soothe those insulted attributes with his lips and tongue. Perhaps even his teeth as well.

But that was the lunacy once again, which seemed to dog him with increased determination with every moment that passed in her presence. And whilst he was most certainly teetering on the brink of madness, given his reckless decision to bring her here, he also had a far more noble force propelling him. He needed to find Aidan, and he had reason to believe he was at last closer to doing so.

"I have fooled many, many people on innumerable occasions," she said with the airs of a duchess. "I always dress thus when Aidan takes me to bare-knuckle boxing matches."

Even his mother would have been impressed with her regal poise, dubious lineage aside. Admiration, however, was decidedly unwelcome when directed toward Miss Sutton. He quashed it with ruthless determination, reminding himself that she had just announced his brother had squired her about London.

Had Aidan kissed her too?

Had she responded in the same manner?

Damn it to hell, what was the matter with him?

He busied himself by lighting some sconces, bringing more light flickering to life. "My brother has been accompanying you to bare-knuckle matches whilst you are dressed as an unconvincing gentleman?"

Did the woman not appreciate how irregular this entire affair was?

"I do believe I spoke plainly." Her tone was tart, a rebuke.

How dare she?

Garrick turned back to her only to discover she was

hovering far too near, her green-brown eyes sparkling even in the shadow cast by her brim, generous lips tilted into the slightest hint of mirth. Of course she dared. Look at her, all that glorious auburn hair somehow piled beneath a monstrosity of a hat, lovelier than the most sought-after demimondaine.

"What did you intend to do with the hat?" he asked, surprising himself with the question.

The answer did not matter. Every moment he tarried here with her was one less spent in more worthy endeavors. And yet, it would seem he could not help himself. He was curious about everything when it came to this woman. What was wrong with him?

Her lips pursed. "The hat?"

His irritation grew, magnified by the desire that had already sparked to life. "The one on your head, madam."

Who was he fooling? The desire had never truly stopped burning. From the moment he had seen her, he had wanted her. Coveted her for himself, regardless of how very wrong such a need was. Regardless of how very wrong *she* was.

"Oh." Her gloved fingers went to the brim, gliding along it. "Keep it on my head, of course. I never had to remove it at the matches."

As he had thought.

"Therein lies the problem, Miss Sutton," he informed her, keeping his voice haughty. "One of many. You were intending to venture into the gaming rooms at The Duke's Bastard whilst wearing a hat. The members of the club all typically remove their outer garments upon entering. Not only would every gentleman within have noticed you for that reason, not a one of them would have been stupid enough to mistake you for a man. Truly, if you are intent upon going about in such a guise, you ought to be intelligent enough to consider no gentleman carries on with his hat upon his head for the entirety of a social event."

Her shoulders stiffened and her chin went up, a posture he recognized now as being defensive. "They do for bare-knuckle boxing."

"Ruffians." His lip curled with distaste. That Aidan would have taken her to such a rough crowd rankled, although Garrick knew it should not. "One hardly ought to consider the actions of an assortment of lewd and rough characters at a bare-knuckle bout the harbinger of polite society."

"Thank you for the lesson, Lord Lordly." She crossed her arms over her sadly flattened breasts and pinned him with a narrow-eyed glare. "Now, if you don't mind, I'm a busy woman. I haven't the time to dawdle with you in the house where you keep your ladybirds." She paused and gave an exaggerated sniff of the air. "None of them are about this evening, are they? I don't smell perfume."

Not again with the *Lord Lordly* business. He absolutely despised when she called him that, and Miss Sutton knew it. Which was why she used the name at every possible opportunity. And *how* had she known Letitia had always been surrounded by a cloud of perfume? Further, how had she understood the manner of residence to which he had brought her?

She was an intelligent woman, Miss Penelope Sutton. A force to be reckoned with. He had known it from the start, but he understood it more now, standing here with her in the place he had vowed never to return when he had bid his farewell to his mistress and given her the congé.

"I advise you to speak to me with greater respect, madam," he bit out, tamping down the urge to kiss those mocking lips.

"Or what shall you do?" she taunted, a teasing smile curving her mouth.

Kiss you.

Bed you.

"I shall make certain none of my friends and acquaintances patronize your family's establishment," he said instead.

The smile fled her lips. "Are you threatening me, Lord Lordly? I would have thought you'd realized your empty promises don't frighten me by now."

How brazen she was.

"It is not empty," he assured her silkily. "Nor is it a threat. I brought you here to speak with you about my brother. Such discourse is naturally best undertaken where no one else is lurking about with eager ears, all the better to spread scandalous gossip."

"Then let's have done with it." She pouted, tapping her booted foot on the floor. "I've places to be."

She had *places to be*.

Where?

And with whom?

He forced his ridiculous jealousy down, harnessing his ire instead. "Curse you, woman. Do you not have a civil tongue inside that stubborn head of yours?"

Her smile was beautiful, transforming her features even beneath that dreadful hat, and lighting a fire within him that made him briefly lightheaded. "Not for you, I don't."

There was no more maddening wench in all England, he was certain of it. And yet, there remained that ludicrous, all-consuming hunger for her he could not seem to quell, regardless of how much he tried with ration, calm, and the stern reminder of how socially inferior she was in every way that mattered.

And all the ways which didn't.

Unfortunately, a certain portion of his anatomy did not

give a damn about anything other than Penelope Sutton's bewitching lips and swaying hips.

He cleared his throat, irritated more than he wished to admit by the sight of that oversized hat hiding her lustrous hair from view. Before he could garner control of himself, he reached out, plucking the offensive monstrosity from her head and tossing it to the floor, where it landed with an ignominious thump.

Her outrage was instant. "What do you think you are doing, throwing about my bleeding hat?"

Ah.

How interesting.

Apparently, when her ire was sufficiently piqued, Miss Sutton's East End roots rose to the surface. Garrick ought to be appalled. Instead, he found himself intrigued. "It was distracting me. I cannot speak with you when half your face is cloaked in shadows."

In truth, he could. But he did not wish to.

Her glorious hair had been restrained with what had to be handfuls of pins, trapped neatly to her head with a carefully coiled chignon pinned high with the obvious intention of being hidden within the accommodating height of the hat.

"Speak to me without it then," she said with a resigned sigh. "You have wasted enough of my time this evening."

Someone ought to remind the vexing woman she should address a viscount with at least a hint of respect. And he would have been the one to inform her, were it not for the undeniable burden of the news he was about to impart. Strangely, the notion of hurting this irritating, burdensome, beautiful woman cut into his heart with the precision of a freshly honed dagger.

"I spoke with one of Aidan's friends at The Duke's Bastard this evening," he forced himself to say, attempting to remain stalwart. "I also managed to have a brief dialogue with Mr. Duncan Kirkwood, who is the owner of the establishment. The information they both shared suggests my brother was—*is*—involved intimately with another…woman."

He had been about to say *another lightskirt*, but that word hardly seemed fitting in relation to Miss Sutton. Despite what he knew of her. *Lady* was not the proper term, either, but to suggest anything less seemed akin to paying the most grievous of insults to the hazel-eyed spitfire before him. *Blast.* What was this? He was considering Miss Sutton's feelings?

Why?

How?

He was certain he ought not. She was hardly deserving of his consideration. After all, she had manipulated his idiotic sibling into this nonsensical betrothal, had she not?

"Another woman?" Miss Sutton repeated, her full lips pursing.

Begging to be kissed, that mouth.

Christ.

Why did she not seem as utterly crushed as she ought to at the news his brother had disappeared with another woman? But then, why had she responded to Garrick's kisses in the manner she had? The woman was convoluted. Perplexing. Vexing.

His cock was painfully hard.

Bringing her here had been a mistake.

Concentrate on the matter at hand, you arse!

Garrick inhaled swiftly, which proved a dreadful misstep as it only brought the delightful scent of Miss Sutton's Winter's soap into his lungs to further tempt him and did nothing to calm his madly surging desires. "Another woman," he said stupidly, watching her for a trace of sadness. For a reaction.

Any.

She remained stoic, nary a trace of sadness on her countenance. "That would hardly be surprising. Each time the wind blows, Aidan finds a new ladybird."

Garrick frowned. "You are not distressed by this knowledge?"

Her lush lips curved upward. "Should I be?"

"As his betrothed, yes," he bit out. "Surely you have some sense of pride, madam."

"Aye, I've pride." She inclined her head, studying him with that regard he continued to find distressingly attractive. "Lots of it. I'm a Sutton, Lord Lordly. We wear our pride on our coat sleeves." Grinning, she offered him her forearm as example.

He examined the coat—a terrible piece of workmanship if he had ever seen one, fashioned from dreadful cloth, altogether too large for her form, the cut and color unbecoming...

What the devil was he thinking? Her coat hardly mattered.

"I should think you would be more concerned, considering your... *betrothal* to my brother," he said stiffly, wishing his prick to the ethers.

His trousers had reached beyond the point of being uncomfortably snug. His self-loathing only slightly eclipsed his insufferable lust.

"He ain't my betrothed."

Her dulcet voice scarcely permeated his vacillating thoughts.

For a moment, Garrick was certain he must have misheard her.

But no. His ears had not deceived him. Her stubborn expression told him so.

"He is not your betrothed?" he repeated, mind racing in

an effort to comprehend this sudden development.

When had they put an end to it? And when had she seen Aidan last? Most importantly of all, why the devil had she not said something sooner?

"No." She shook her head, a hint of sheepishness entering her gaze before she blinked, those long lashes lowering to chase the emotion. "He ain't. He never was."

Now, he was convinced he was mistaken. "Forgive me, Miss Sutton. I must beg you to repeat what you just said."

"You heard me correctly, Lord Lordly. I was never going to marry your brother. He didn't even propose. He came to me with this nonsensical notion we ought to wed to spite your father. I told him to go to the devil, but apparently he misunderstood me, for he went to your family with the news we were betrothed instead."

Garrick stared at her, his mind gradually drinking in this new knowledge. He ought to be experiencing a number of emotions, shock and outrage primary amongst them. However, as he beheld the woman who had been the object of his furious desires from the instant he had first seen her, all he felt was a searing, delirious, almost dizzying sense of relief.

Relief he had not been kissing his brother's betrothed.

That he had not been lusting after her like a besotted fool, betraying Aidan.

That he would not have to explain to Father and Mother that he had been unsuccessful in his attempts at persuading Miss Sutton not to snap their youngest son in the parson's mousetrap because he, as their eldest, had been thrusting his tongue down her throat at every opportunity.

And relief because if she was not betrothed to his brother, that meant Garrick could have her for himself.

Thank God.

"You are not marrying my brother," he said slowly.

"You are a clever nob, aren't you?"

Whether it was her biting sarcasm, the smirk curving her pretty lips, or the reassurance she was not Aidan's betrothed that motivated him, he could not say. All he did know was that in the next moment, his body was moving, surrendering to his desires, taking control over his mind.

He snaked an arm around her waist and pulled her flush against him, and then he claimed her mouth with his.

OF ALL THE responses she had anticipated receiving from the viscount when she revealed to him Aidan was not her betrothed, seduction had not been among them. And yet, that was precisely what was happening now.

His lips were demanding, hot and firm and giving her no choice but to kiss him in return. How could she not? She would never understand her weakness for the arrogant man holding her so snugly in his arms—as if she were somehow dear to him.

What a lark! In truth, she knew she was anything but. He had made his disdain for her quite apparent. She was not fit to marry his younger brother, and he had been willing to bribe her in order to avoid the terrible scandal which would have ensued had he and his lofty duke and duchess parents been forced to welcome her into the family. Why, then, these passionate kisses? Why his tongue teasing her lips to open, then delving inside?

He tasted of sweetness and mystery, and regardless of all the reasons why she should not, Pen longed for Viscount Lindsey. Longed for him badly.

Longed for him more than she had ever desired a man's kisses and touches before.

Perhaps this was her reward for taunting him. She should

not have goaded him, and she knew it, but as he deepened the kiss and moved them slowly backward, she could not summon a hint of regret. Because she was aflame, and he was nipping at her lower lip as if he wanted to consumer her, and her frantically beating heart and the need burning through her told her that she wanted to devour him too.

It made no sense.

They despised each other.

He was an arse who believed the worst of her, always polished to polite societal perfection.

But an arse who melted her defiance, it was true.

Somehow, her hair pins were raining to the floor and her hair, previously trapped in the tightest chignon she could muster, spilled in heavy waves down her back. His mouth left hers to find the side of her throat, the patch of skin above her rudely tied cravat. His breath fanned over her desperate flesh, making her knees cease to hold their stern shape. They buckled.

He caught her, hauling her into his arms.

Of course he did. Lord Lordly was faultless elegance in every act he committed. A gentleman like him would never allow a lady—even one he looked down his aristocratic nose at—to fall. She wanted to summon resentment, anything to resurrect her swiftly crumbling defenses, and found none.

But then, he quite startled her. Because he was *carrying* her in his deliciously strong arms. Carrying her through the dimly lit hall into the darkness beyond, holding her tightly to his chest as the scent of him wound its way through her senses. Citrus and bay and musk in a combination that rendered her nearly delirious with desire.

The house was empty. And thank heavens for that. But he knew his way, and she should have been bothered by the knowledge, just as she should have resisted his lips and rejected his kisses. Just as she should not be here with him now, very much in danger of losing whatever lingering remnants of her tattered virtue remained.

Yet, she was not bothered. And she was here. And if she did indeed lose the ragged shreds of her virtue to the viscount, she knew she would not grieve a single bit of them.

"My God," he said against her throat, "why do I want you so bloody much? I have asked myself again and again, and yet I can find no answer."

She would have answered him, but she had been asking herself the same question ever since he had first kissed her, and then again just moments ago. Pen most certainly did not have the answer. She doubted she ever would.

It ceased to matter anyway.

He had moved them over a threshold. Light from the brace of candles he had lit in the hall carried dimly over, sending shadows and a warm glow to dance around them. A brief glimpse of carpets and furniture suggested the chamber was a room for receiving callers.

He settled her on a large French sofa, falling to his knees on the carpet as he went, nudging her legs apart so he could settle between her thighs.

He was a tall man, his height such that even in his current position, their faces were at the same level. For a bewildering moment, their gazes met and held before he made a sound of raw desire in his throat and his lips were on hers in a deep, drugging kiss.

What was it about this man's lips that made her want to feel them on hers without end? Their tongues mated, and she knew in that instant that she was going to give herself to him. Not because he was a vaunted lord, the heir to a duke. But because she wanted him. She wanted him, and Pen had never been saving herself for marriage. She had no interest in taking a husband. Why not allow herself this reckless moment of abandon? Men did so all the time, and without recrimination.

He broke the kiss and dragged his mouth along her jaw. Her head fell back in invitation.

"You are bewitching." His low voice was at her ear, his teeth nipping her lobe as his fingers made short work of the knot of her cravat.

Oh good heavens, yes. Yes, yes, yes.

The lone word became a litany in her mind as he flung the scrap of linen to the floor. And again as he undid the handful of buttons at the neck of her shirt. More acquiescence hummed through her veins while he peeled her out of her coat and waistcoat, and then pulled her shirt over her head.

He lowered his head to kiss her shoulder while his large, warm hands cupped her breasts through the binding she had wrapped around them earlier that evening before setting out on her jaunt. She never could have predicted this outcome then. His teeth emerged to graze along her clavicle until she shivered.

"What have you done?" he asked, his thumbs unerringly finding her nipples beneath the layers of fabric she had used to secure herself. "Such a travesty."

The combined effect of his touch and the tightness of the linen had her aching. She wanted his hands and mouth on her. Without thought, she found the pins keeping the binding in place. She plucked them free, and though she knew she ought to place them somewhere for safekeeping, his hot gaze on her was enough to make her forget.

They slipped from her touch, raining to the carpet below.

Holding his stare, she began to unravel the linen. With each layer that came undone, her heart sped, the desire coursing through her burning hotter, anticipation sparking to life like a flame. The last of the binding fell to her lap, leaving her breasts bare. Relief and desire warred for supremacy.

His head dipped, his breath fanning hotly over her aching flesh, and desire won. When his mouth latched on to the peak of her breast, she nearly came out of her skin. He sucked. Liquid heat pooled between her thighs. This longing was familiar and yet new. New because it was stronger than anything she had ever experienced.

"Christ, you are perfection," he praised against the swell of her breast. "It hardly seems fair."

No, she was not perfect at all. He was. And yes, she thoroughly agreed that it was most unfair. She would have said as much aloud had he not then taken her other nipple into his mouth. And had not his hands caressed her waist so tenderly, as if even her skin was a vessel to be worshipped, learning the curves in a slow way that suggested he was committing them to his memory.

Her hands, previously occupied by clasping the silken tufted cushions of the luxurious sofa, reached for his broad shoulders now instead. His heat was a welcome sear, but it occurred to her that there were far too many layers of gentility keeping her from what she wanted.

Him.

A new boldness seized her, and she pushed at his shoulders until he rocked back, his gaze melding with hers. "Shall I stop?"

Ah, he believed she was putting an end to this interlude.

"If you do, I'll plant you a facer, Lord Lordly."

His smile was instant and genuine. So genuine, it quite caught her by surprise.

Heavens, the viscount was handsome. Diabolically so.

"Garrick," he said.

For a moment, she blinked at him in befuddlement, trying to comprehend the meaning.

"My name," he added, his voice somehow...softer, having lost some of the crisp aristocratic starch he ordinarily wielded like a weapon. "You may use it, if you like."

He was giving her permission to use his given name. Her heart thudded hard.

"Garrick," she repeated, liking it far too much on her tongue. She swallowed, trying to chase the inconvenient emotions persisting. Desire was all she would allow herself to feel for him. "You may call me Pen."

"Pen."

Her name in his baritone made a wicked thrum of need pulse to life at her core. For a heartbeat, all she could manage was to stare at the arrogant lord who had believed the worst of her when he had first appeared at The Sinner's Palace. Who perhaps still did.

And yet, he was on his knees before her.

She wanted to see what was hidden beneath his aristocratic layers. Needed to. She reached for his coat, and he aided her in shucking the garment, along with his waistcoat. His cravat came next, and they worked together to pull his shirt over his head.

Shadows and light flickered over him as he moved, lovingly illuminating and then hiding the contours of his broad chest. What a marvel his clothing had been hiding. He took her breath. She was reaching for him again without conscious thought, her palms coasting over his warm skin, following muscle and sinew to the waistband of his trousers.

He made a new sound, laden with such raw need, she would have fallen to her knees herself were she not already seated before him. Whatever Viscount Lindsey thought of her, despite the disparity in their stations, he wanted her. His words had told her one tale, and the rest of him was telling another. For the first time, he was not invulnerable.

When her right hand paused over his wildly beating heart, she had no doubt of it.

"Pen," he repeated, his voice a delicious rasp to her senses. But when those sculpted lips would have said more, she pressed her fingers to them, staying his words.

His mouth stretched into a smile beneath her touch, and he tipped his head back, kissing her fingers before sucking one into his mouth. The silken, wet heat and the suction sent a peculiar rush of need through her, the gesture intimate and erotic all at once.

Holding her gaze in the dim light, he released the digit he had been torturing to kiss a path up her inner wrist. He caressed her thighs in slow, knowing strokes, thumbs pressing lightly into the delicate flesh. He stopped at her elbow, his head lifting, the new angle allowing the flickering candelabra from the nearby hall to catch on his sharp cheekbones and haughty brows.

She was melting. Falling. Desiring.

Being foolish as she had been before, it was true.

But she was older now. Wiser, she liked to believe. And besides, when a woman's heart had already been broken, there were only pieces remaining. Nothing left to shatter any more, since it had been ground to dust beneath Daniel's boot heel.

The thought of the man she had so recklessly believed herself in love with was enough to propel Pen into action. She hooked her legs around Lord Lindsey's waist and pulled him onto the generous sofa with her. He went willingly, easily, falling atop her whilst taking care to keep his weight from crushing her into the tufted silk cushions and abundance of pillows adorning the piece of furniture.

His scent encircled her, and so did his heat, his strength. The evidence of how badly he desired her was pressed thick and hard against her where she ached the most. As if to prove just how much they wanted each other, he swiveled his hips, bringing the lower halves of their bodies into delicious, grinding connection.

"I did not bring you here for this," he said.

Even if he had, she was beyond the point of caring. The two of them had been dancing about each other from the moment their paths had first clashed. In some ways, it was inevitable that they found themselves thus.

"But you want it now," she finished for him, her hips chasing his as he rocked against her.

She knew what the act of making love entailed. Although any one of her brothers would have torn Daniel Peabody limb from bloody limb if they had discovered what had happened when Pen had been sixteen, that long-ago time when she had believed herself in love with him had made certain she possessed a rudimentary understanding. But although years had passed and time had faded her memory, she knew she had never felt this wildly wanton. The feelings and sensations she had known before were a tepid comparison.

"I want it," the viscount—Garrick—said, bringing her mind from the murky depths of a past best left in the dark. "I want you."

Another slow roll of his hips.

And she was wet and aching.

"Then have me," she invited, shamelessly pressing her breasts into his chest as she arched her back. Her nipples were hard and eager to be touched. Her entire body was aflame.

This was his fault. He alone had caused this madness, and now he had to put an end to it for the both of them. There could be no other outcome to this night save one.

"Have you," he repeated in a dangerous voice.

One that was sinful and husky and promised delirious passion.

"Yes." The need was rising up from a new place within her, and with it came a sense of power she had never known. She was no stranger to men looking upon her with rampant desire. Each night she had donned a wig and sung for the patrons of The Sinner's Palace, she had watched the fancy nobs as they looked on, longing for the illusion she had presented them.

But Lord Lindsey was different. He did not desire the blonde wig or the saucy singer, not the role she had played. No, indeed. He wanted plain Pen Sutton, the fiery-haired daughter of a drunkard, who had lived in the East End all her life. Who sometimes dropped an *h* and spoke flash despite the efforts her eldest brother had gone to so that she would speak like a lady. Garrick desired her not because of what and who she was, ready to take advantage of her, but rather in spite of it. And somehow, that made a difference to Pen.

That made *all* the difference.

He stilled, dipping his head to rest his forehead against hers, his breath fanning across her mouth in the most delicious prelude to a kiss she had ever experienced. "This is a mistake."

She froze, thwarted desire sending a waterfall of disappointment to douse the flames of her desire. But before she could say a word, his mouth was on hers. He was kissing her again. Deeply, hotly, deliciously. Kissing her as if his next breath depended upon the precise manner in which he moved his lips against hers.

His hand slipped between them, working meticulously on the fall of her trousers. Buttons slid from moorings. Fabric parted. His tongue was in her mouth. And then, the miracle of his touch, stroking there, where she wanted him most. Where her flesh was throbbing and longing for his touch.

He lifted his head, breaking the kiss, his breathing harsh. "Christ. You are dripping."

As if to punctuate his words, he worked his fingers over her folds in slow, steady thrusts. The wet sounds seemed to echo in the hushed silence of the house. There was nothing between them but the steady rise and fall of their breaths and the sound of him teasing her.

When he parted her folds and he found the sensitive bud hidden within, her hips bucked and she cried out.

He toyed with her, circling her nub and then delving deeper, finding her cunny. He probed her with his middle finger, and then he lowered his head to suck her nipple as he thrust into her with that lone digit. The invasion was new, unexpected.

Good.

So good.

Better than good. What was better than good? The best. *Lord in heaven and all the angels, yes.* He was the best.

She arched into his touch, bringing him deeper.

His attentions were so different from what she had come to expect, from what she knew. She felt as if she were stretched full of him, and yet simultaneously as if she did not have nearly enough. There was no pain, no discomfort, no pinching. Instead, her body felt as if it were made for his. He thrust in and out gently, slowly at first, and then with increasing vigor as his tongue lashed her nipples.

When his thumb circled over her pearl as his other finger sank deep, the combination proved too much. He sucked hard on the peak of her breast, thrusting inside her as his thumb stroked and strummed and brought her to release. The sheer pleasure of it nearly tore her apart. She felt as if she were wound tightly and then exploded into the ether, such delicious abandon and pleasure swamping her body and mind that she was helpless to do anything but ride his hand, hips tipping greedily upward for more, and hold his handsome face to her breasts so that he would continue this sweet torture.

Her heart was pounding so hard and so fast as the desire licked through her that she feared it would burst. But as the waves of her crisis ebbed, the pounding continued.

And that was when she realized it was not her heart at all.

Rather, it was someone rapping on the door.

CHAPTER 7

He had committed an egregious mistake. A bloody stupid, reckless, pointless misstep.

Nearly tupping his brother's—Christ, not betrothed, but what to call her? His brother's... No. Garrick refused to think of her as anything in relation to Aidan now. Not after he had stroked her silken quim until she had come. She would forever be Pen to him now.

Still, nearly fucking her on a French sofa in a darkened drawing room had not been one of his finer moments. As he threw his shirt over his head and hastened to stuff it into the waistband of his trousers whilst someone continued a barrage upon the front door, he knew a searing, stinging shame.

"Whoever this is, he had bloody well be about to tell me the world is coming to an end," he grumbled, as irritated by the interruption as he was with himself and his utter lack of restraint.

Pen was scrambling to right her garments as well, and scoundrel that he was, he could not resist chancing another glance at her full breasts swaying with her frantic motions.

Her pretty pink nipples were still deliciously hard, and keeping himself from taking a stiff peak into his mouth required all the restraint he possessed.

Rap rap rap.

The unknown presence at the door continued to make himself known in loud, irritating fashion.

"I will return," he told Pen, having shrugged into his coat. His cravat was missing, and his waistcoat had been thrown somewhere into the murk. This was his best effort at appearing as if he had not just been about to shag a thoroughly inappropriate woman he had no business desiring, let alone touching.

She nodded, and for reasons he cared not to examine, the fact that she had remained silent in the aftermath of her crisis nettled him. He wished she would say something—anything. Perhaps even a caustic *Lord Lordly* would be welcome. It would certainly do to quell his aching prick and the memory of her, all sleek and pulsing and tight, clamping on his finger.

If only it had been his cock.

Rap rap rap.

"Do not go anywhere," he added for good measure, his throat suddenly thickened by thwarted desire.

Still, she said nothing, her small hands working to restore her clothing into a semblance of order. Grinding his jaw, he turned and stalked from the room, intent upon answering the door and putting an end to this damned nonsense. What a lark—a viscount, answering the door as if he were a butler. And in such a state of dishabille. But there wasn't any other help for it. He had dismissed the staff some time ago, and there was no one else about.

Rap rap rap.

He threw open the door, determined to put the bastard in his place. But the man standing at the threshold, presumably responsible for all the noise, was a familiar face. His coachman, as it happened.

"Neave?"

"Begging your pardon for the interruption, my lord," said his ordinarily impeccable retainer, breathless and wild-eyed and quite unlike himself.

"What is amiss?" he demanded, concern curdling his gut.

"It's Lord Aidan, Lord Lindsey."

Aidan? His stomach lurched with a combination of relief and upset. "Where the devil is he?"

And why here, why now? Why could he not have appeared hours earlier, before Garrick had made such a muck of everything?

"I can't say, my lord." Neave held out a missive which had been neatly folded. "A scamp in the mews gave this to me without a word and ran off. I read it, thinking it was for me. But it seems as if Lord Aidan is being held for ransom."

Ransom?

Aidan?

With a trembling hand, Garrick took the missive, unfolding it and hastily reading its concise contents.

Find Lord Aidan Weir by delivering one thousand pounds to the alley behind The Beggar's Purse tomorrow evening at half past ten. Tell no one if you value his life.

It was unsigned.

His fist clenched on the words, crumpling them.

Could it be true? Had his reckless brother somehow fallen into the clutches of villains who were now using him as a pawn to secure a small fortune for themselves?

"The scamp who delivered this to you in the mews," he said slowly, trying to force his overburdened mind to make sense of the situation at hand. "What did he look like?"

Neave shook his head. "I am sorry, my lord. He was in the shadows, and it happened with such haste…I never imagined the importance of the missive the lad handed over, or I would have apprehended him. He was no more than twelve, I would say, with hair that was perhaps dark in color."

Damn it. The coachman could have been describing anyone.

But this was not Neave's fault. If Aidan had indeed been kidnapped by thieves, he was entirely to blame for his stupid, wild carousing and his lack of respect for every virtue Father had instilled in them and…

Her.

Garrick's eyes narrowed as a new suspicion set in. The sum mentioned in the missive was twice the amount he had offered Pen to break off the engagement. A betrothal which she had just insisted never existed in the first place. Was it possible she was attempting to secure an even greater fortune from his family than that which had already been offered?

And meanwhile, Garrick had been sucking at her breasts, his hand shoved down her trousers, making her spend like the scoundrel he apparently was. What power she held over him. He would have to put an end to it.

"You are not to blame, and nor do you have a need to apologize," he reassured his worried-looking coachman. "You could not have known what the missive contained or why the lad had sought you out. Thank you for bringing the matter to my attention, that it may be speedily dealt with. Bring the carriage around, if you please. I will be returning my friend to his club in the East End before traveling home."

Yes, referring to Pen as his male *friend* rendered him peevish. Especially since he was standing before his coachman looking as if he had just been involved in libidinous behavior. Which he had. But not with his gentleman friend.

Friend was the last appellation he would apply to Pen Sutton.

"Of course, milord," said the coachman, who took his leave with a bow.

Garrick closed the door against the cool air of the night and took a moment to compose himself. So many emotions were roiling through him at once that his mind was nothing more than a thick, churning stew of anger, lust, confusion, and fear. He had been about to lose himself with Pen, it was true. The timing of the interruption could not have been better.

Or, it could have been planned.

Either way, there was no denying that Aidan had been missing these last few days. If he had indeed been taken against his will and was being held somewhere, Garrick would stop at nothing to rescue his brother and see him safely returned. And if Miss Penelope Sutton had anything to do with what had befallen Aidan, vengeance would be his.

She would be the one paying.

He turned and stalked back to the drawing room, this time bringing the brace of candles with him. Light flickered over the chamber, chasing the shadows which had drenched it and rendered it so intimate previously. It was just as he remembered, the furniture having been chosen and artfully arranged by his former mistress. And in the midst of it all stood Pen Sutton, as out of place as a cat floating in the River Thames.

She did not belong here. But damn it, she was the most beautiful woman he had ever beheld, even dressed as she was, in the poorest attempt at mimicking a gentleman he had ever beheld.

Those hips.

Christ.

Cease thinking of her hips, you daft fool. And her lips for that matter. And how wet she had been.

"What is in your hand?" she asked, her gaze dropping to his fist, which was still clenched around the unwanted communication.

"A missive from someone who has apparently apprehended my brother and is demanding one thousand pounds in return for him," he ground out, clinging to his suspicion and his outrage. Those were far safer than the longing and desire, after all. He tried to summon an image of Lady Hester to his mind and failed dismally. "Tell me, Miss Sutton, what do you have to do with this latest farce?"

Her eyes were wide. "Someone has Aidan?"

"*Lord* Aidan," he corrected, because he still disliked the informal nature with which she referred to his brother.

He felt ridiculously possessive when it came to this woman. Obviously, he was going to have to do something to rectify this terrible state of affairs.

"As if his title matters at a time like this," she said, waving a dismissive hand in the air as if to suggest *he* were the one at fault.

"It matters." He cleared his throat, thoroughly irritated with her and still battling a most inconvenient surge of attraction brought about by the swaying of her breasts beneath that cursed shirt. Why had she not bound herself again? Her nipples were erect, prodding the thin cambric. "But do cease your attempts at distraction. They ill become you. I shall ask you again, and if you do not answer me, I must warn you I'll not be nearly as polite the next time I ask. What do you know of this, madam?"

Her brows arched, and she crossed her arms over her chest in a defensive posture, mercifully hiding her breasts from his avid gaze. "I know nothing of it, Lord Lordly. Why should I?"

"Why should you not?" he countered. "You have spent an inordinate amount of time with Lord Aidan recently. You orchestrated a fictional betrothal with him, one which your conscience apparently finally forced you to admit was a falsehood, and when one Weir brother was not available, you simply seduced another."

The moment the last accusation left him, Garrick wished he could have recalled it. He took no pleasure in the way she flinched as if he had struck her. But then, her shoulders went back and her chin tipped up, and with her hair flowing down her back, she resembled nothing so much as an avenging goddess of war.

An enraged one.

"Is that what you truly believe, my lord?" she demanded, ice in her voice.

Yes, it was. Was it not?

He searched himself for the answer and realized it was not one he wished to know.

He sighed. "Do you or do you not have any knowledge of where my brother has gone or has been taken?"

She had claimed ignorance before, but he scarcely knew what to believe or think at this juncture. He had been torn apart with lust for a woman he had previously reviled, and now his brother was potentially being held captive by mercenaries who may or may not have been hired at her whim.

"As I have already told you on numerous occasions, I have no notion of where he has gone. If what you say is true and he has been taken captive, however, lingering here to pay me further insults will not do him one whit of good." Her gaze was withering, her tone possessing the stinging bite of a cracking whip.

Blast her, but she was not wrong.

"You are correct that lingering here will not aid my brother," he said, agreeing with her as a plan took shape in his mind. "That is why the carriage is being brought around as we speak."

She nodded. "For once, you are exhibiting common sense. I commend you, my lord. I'll just be dressing, and then I will show myself out and hire a hack home."

The hell she would.

"You will be accompanying me, my dear," he informed her before turning his attention to the room itself.

His damned cravat and waistcoat were somewhere within, and he had no wish to gad about without having first donned them. Never let it be said that the exalted Viscount Lindsey had been in a state of unfashionable disarray. He would find the deuced cravat and waistcoat if it proved the death of him.

"I wouldn't accompany you to heaven if you claimed to be the Lord himself," she told him stubbornly, her slim arms still crossed in a defiant pose.

He ought to have been relieved at the manner in which she kept him from ogling her breasts. But the truth was, he was every bit the raging reprobate he had always accused Aidan of being. The need to see, touch, and taste her again was as overwhelming as the worry he felt for his brother and whatever coil Aidan had landed himself in.

"You have not got a choice in the matter," he informed the arrogant Miss Sutton. "You will go where I say you go."

Her hazel eyes narrowed. "You do not tell me what to do, Lord Lordly. I do what I want, when I want to do it, and not because any man tells me. Not even a lofty viscount such as yournabs."

Yournabs.

At times, it was appallingly easy—likely because she had been somehow tutored in the art of masking her dreadful accent—to forget she was an East End lady. But here was an alarming reminder of who he was lusting after. He ought to be appalled with himself in more ways than he dared to count. But that did not stop him from wanting her more than he desired to take his next breath. Even whilst Aidan was missing and possibly in the clutches of some villainous madmen. Even whilst Garrick suspected her of being a part of the plot, or perhaps worse.

"You are going to help me find my brother and bring him home," he informed her. "I do not believe you when you claim you aren't involved. There are far too many coincidences for me to believe otherwise. A fortune hunter such as yourself would not stop at five hundred pounds, would she? Not when she could have one thousand instead, and perhaps even the heir instead of the spare. Is that why you have been throwing yourself into my arms at every possible opportunity?"

It would certainly make sense. But a part of him loathed the notion of her wanting him for any reason other than the same mad desire he felt for her.

"Throwing myself into your arms?" she repeated, her tone indignant. "Of all the conceited, ridiculous, pompous, arrogant, arsehole remarks to have emerged from your smug lordly lips, surely that statement is the worst. Certainly, it is the most insulting."

He was being beastly, and even he could admit as much to himself. But he would be damned if he would make such a concession to her. He owed her nothing. He had given her pleasure, and she had given him aching ballocks and a cockstand he could do nothing to assuage. And then there was the self-loathing, which rivaled the size of England itself, festering within him.

How could he long for her so when he did not trust her, and when she was the most unsuitable female he had ever known, and when she was somehow entangled with his own brother? It made no sense.

"What would you have from me, madam?" he demanded, stalking past her to rescue his pathetically rumpled cravat from beneath a chair. "An apology? All you have done from the moment you first insinuated yourself into my brother's life is to make trouble." He snatched up the cravat and rose to his full height, turning back to her with a scowl. "First this betrothal folderol, then his sudden disappearance, followed by your hoydenish behavior."

"Hoydenish, is it?" Her arms were uncrossed and planted on her hips now, which meant that her nipples, still prodding the soft fabric of her white shirt, were taunting him. As were the full mounds of her breasts, swaying as her dudgeon increased. "I ought to darken your day lights for saying such a despicable thing to me."

Some part of him—a peculiar part to be sure—found her defiance intriguing. Appealing, even. But the rest of him—the part that had been sternly and steadfastly raised to bring credit to the family line as the future Duke of Dryden—was appalled that she would dare to threaten him with bodily harm after already having struck him on a previous occasion. He had thought they were beyond such foolishness.

Garrick tried to envision Lady Hester in a similar situation and failed. Curse it, he could not even seem to recall the color of her eyes at the moment. He was so absorbed in the hazel gaze of the spitfire before him that everything else ceased to exist.

Aidan, he reminded himself. *Your stupid, foolish, addle-pated, ne'er-do-well brother needs you.*

"I dare you to attempt it," he forced himself to tell Miss Sutton. "You are more than welcome to try."

By now, Neave would be awaiting them in front of the house. Lingering here with her was not just idiotic but a waste of precious time as well. He made short work of a knot and then took off his coat so that he could don his waistcoat.

All the while, she watched him silently, that stare of hers following his every movement. Judging him, it seemed. But neither had she moved in an attempt to follow through with her warnings, so he likely ought to deem this a victory.

"You aren't worth bloodying my knuckles again, Lord Lordly," she said.

He should not have allowed those words to burrow past his defenses, but he did.

He turned back to find her winding her hair into its former chignon using whatever pins she must have scavenged from the floor. What a pity to watch those long, wavy locks disappearing. However, the action did force her breasts to rise high and full against the front of her shirt.

He forgot to breathe as he recalled those sensitive buds in his mouth, beneath his tongue. She was so wonderfully responsive and genuine in her desire. Other women he had known in the past had always possessed an air of cunning calculation. When one was engaged in a business transaction with another, passion could scarcely be trusted. But Pen Sutton writhing beneath him had been nothing short of heavenly. He would never forget this night, no matter how hard he tried, and likely, he would be damned to hell for all eternity for it.

"I shall consider myself fortunate," he drawled in mocking fashion.

It was the sort of cutting rejoinder he might have issued in the drawing room or on the ballroom floor to let a social enemy know they were impinging upon his patience and grace. In polite society, the approval of Viscount Lindsey could make any man or woman. But the disapproval could break him or her just as well.

He was equally revered and feared.

Only Miss Penelope Sutton failed to appreciate the immensity of his stature, mocking him and taking a stand against him at every turn, and when she had no damned right to do so. She was infuriating.

The most beautiful, intoxicating creature he had ever known.

Lady Hester could not possibly compare, and nor could the woman who had once inhabited these four walls. But it was hardly a competition, was it? And nor did it matter.

"You do that, Lord Lordly," came her taunting voice, slicing through his thoughts. "And while you're going about it, tell yourself I'm the one who seduced you. Tell yourself I'm the one who slipped her hand down your trousers and stroked your—"

"Enough," he ground out, needing to put an end to her words, for fear the effect they were having upon him.

He needed to think of Aidan. To find his brother. Not to continue dallying with this cursed female.

"Why can you not admit it?" she queried softly.

He should not ask her what she was speaking of. He ought to be shepherding her to the damned door. Instead, he was lingering in this world of mystery and shadow and iniquity, where he had nearly taken her as his. Where he wanted to take her still, despite all reason and logic and honor.

"Admit what?" His attempt at scoffing was rendered nebulous by the hitch in his breath.

Lord, how much further could he lower himself into the pit of disreputable deeds?

She sauntered nearer, exuding confidence that was entirely deserved. If she but crooked her finger, he would be on his knees for her.

"That you desire me, Garrick. You desire me, and you loathe yourself for that weakness. You are accustomed to living a life that is always above reproach. How dare your body betray you with something so base and unwanted as physical need for a woman you have deemed so hopelessly your inferior? That is how you feel, is it not?"

His thoughts teemed, scrambling and tripping over themselves. How despicable she made him sound. And how strange and intimate it was for her to use his Christian name. Who had given her leave to…

He had. In the frenzy of lust which had overtaken him, he had told her to call him Garrick. She had been charming him with her acerbic wit and unparalleled bravado. And so he had bid her use the name scarcely anyone used.

How right it sounded on her lips.

Curse it all. How dare he think Aidan a hen wit when he was no better, falling so easily beneath her spell?

He swallowed. "You know nothing of what you speak, Miss Sutton."

She raised a brow, the expression on her countenance one of sensual knowledge, sending a new arrow of heat directly to his groin. "Oh, I know, Lord Lordly. Trust me. I do."

But that was the trouble, was it not? He did not trust this woman. Nor could he.

Ever.

He was not sure which of them angered him more in that moment, her or himself.

"Finish preparing yourself, madam," he said coolly, attempting to disguise his irritation. "We have tarried here long enough, and my carriage awaits."

Without bothering to wait for her response, he offered her a terse bow and then quit the chamber.

CHAPTER 8

Lord Lordly was in quite a huff.

Pen was not surprised. She knew she had been pressing him too far. But when the tender lover had vanished, replaced by the haughty lord, she had not been able to resist needling him. Her reward was to be bundled rudely into his carriage and secreted to a destination unknown.

She eyed him now, seated opposite her in the swaying conveyance, and could not keep her wicked impulses under control.

Pen nudged his booted foot with hers. "Where are you taking me, Lord Lordly?"

His lips compressed into a disapproving line. "To a place where I can make certain you will not cause me further trouble."

Hmm. The alarm which had been gnawing at her ever since he had claimed he received word that Aidan was being held for ransom by unknown miscreants grew stronger. The heightened concern was as much for herself as for her friend. If he had indeed managed to find himself in such a scrape, she would hardly be surprised. However, she could only imagine what manner of fiend would do something so dastardly. Aidan was forever pockets to let, his vowels scattered about London. Perhaps he had crossed the wrong man.

But regardless of where Aidan was, Pen found herself being held similarly captive. Only, the viscount had not spoken of ransoms.

"You realize, do you not, that my family will come looking for me when I fail to return?" she asked with a calm she did not feel.

Oh, it was not that she feared the man seated opposite her. Nothing he had done thus far gave her cause to suspect he would hurt her. Rather, it was the notion of what her brothers might do, should they discover where she had gone and with whom.

"Let them look as they please," he drawled, his countenance impassive. "It would be little different from the games I am being forced to play with my own brother."

"Yes, but we are not responsible for whatever ill has befallen Aidan," she reminded him.

"*Lord* Aidan," he corrected. "And the matter of whether or not you and your siblings are responsible remains to be seen."

The insufferable oaf.

Had it been a mere hour before that he had been bringing her to the heights of pleasure with his exquisitely knowing touch? It seemed impossible to believe the cold, gruff lord before her was the same ardent lover who had kissed her as if he wanted to consume her.

Pen stifled the urge to kick him in his lordly shin. "You truly believe we have secreted him somewhere and are demanding ransom? Why should we be bothered to do such a thing?"

"You would be able to double your largesse with such an action, would you not? And who better to make your quarry than a reckless blockhead who is always flitting about, drowning himself in petticoats and drink?"

His estimation of Aidan was once more insulting. She would have defended him, but she was feeling rather vexed with her friend at the moment. If he had not insisted upon this wretched, terrible idea of his, she would not be trapped in this carriage with his arrogant brother. And she most definitely would not have kissed him or allowed him to remove various articles of clothing, and she certainly would never have given him liberty to touch her intimately.

Best not to think of such things at the moment.

Aye, that was true.

She pinned her handsome enemy with a glare. "There is a flaw in your logic, Lordly. Hasn't it occurred to you that I've already told you we are not, nor were we ever, betrothed? Therefore, there ain't a need for your blood money to keep me from sullying your family name. I don't want to marry your brother, nor am I holding him prisoner, you conceited lout."

He continued observing her with a dispassionate stare, apparently unmoved. "A lout, am I? You did not seem to think me one earlier."

Heat simmered through her at the reference to what had passed between them in the drawing room. Ruthlessly, she banished it. "And you did not seem to think me a dogged fortune hunter earlier either, or the sort of lady who would take her friend captive and hold him for ransom. Yet, here we are."

"Indeed, here we are." His long fingers strummed lightly on his thigh, as if he were impatient to arrive at their destination.

And likely, he was.

Pen, on the other hand, was not. "Where are you taking me?" she asked again.

Her attempt to evade him at their previous stop had led to the viscount chasing her down the street and catching her, before hauling her over his shoulder and depositing her in his carriage. If his coachman, who had been watching the events unfold, thought it odd for his employer to be running about London with his gentleman friend, he wisely kept silent.

There was only so much resistance one could put up against a man thrice her size. Short of stabbing or shooting him, that was. And she had no desire to find herself in the hulks over the maiming or murder of Lord Lordly. He had caused her enough trouble thus far, thank you.

"To my town house, Miss Sutton."

He was being so formal. And proper.

But she knew what those sculpted aristocratic lips felt like on hers. And on her breasts.

She swallowed, chasing the reminder. "Your town house? You cannot be serious."

The carriage came to a halt.

He inclined his head. "Deadly serious, my dear. Be warned that if you cause me any problems, I shall not hesitate to lock you in the attics."

Ah, so that had not been his original plan.

"You are bringing me to your home as a guest?" she asked.

"The hour is late. I've nowhere else to take you. I have an aching head, my brother is missing, and you vex me mightily."

A shadow passed over his handsome face. Sadness? Irritation? She could not be certain.

"If you are intending to ravish me, I must warn you I will not hesitate to bludgeon you with the nearest sharp object," she told him for good measure.

His lips twitched. "Indeed?"

She nodded. "A fire poker shall do nicely."

He shook his head. "You are the oddest creature, Miss Sutton. Come along. I must decide whether or not I will take this missive to the watch, and I haven't time to remain here, exchanging barbs with you."

"The watch ain't going to do a thing about finding Aidan," she grumbled. "Trust me. Their palms are all being greased, and not by nobs such as yourself."

"You would suggest that, would you not? You would not wish to be caught."

Naturally, he would continue to insist upon clinging to his distrust of her.

She thrust aside the sting of disappointment and brushed past him, descending from the carriage first by leaping from the step and landing on her feet. Unfortunately, her overly large boots made her ankle roll to its side, ensuing pain branding her limb as she toppled forward.

Large, capable hands caught her waist, hauling her against a broad, familiar chest.

"What the devil were you thinking, leaping from the carriage like a tiger springing from a curricle?" he growled. "Have you done yourself injury?"

"Yes." She bit her lip to stifle the pain and corresponding prick of surprised tears.

She would not indulge in a bout of the waterworks before this man. She would show him no weakness.

"Blast you, Pen."

She knew a moment of startled surprise at his use of her given name. But then he further dashed her wits by scooping her into his arms. She clutched at his shoulders for purchase. It was almost as if, for a moment, his façade had slipped. He had forgotten himself. And he was Garrick again, rather than Viscount Lindsey. He was simply a man who had kissed her breathless and brought her exquisite pleasure and scooped her into his arms when she had hurt herself.

What an inconvenient thought to have, and at the worst possible moment, too.

She sniffed and surreptitiously dashed at the evidence of tears with the back of her hand, keeping her eyes on his sharp jawline as he carried her through the mews. "Do you think you ought to be carrying your gentleman friend into your fancy town house, Lord Lordly? Only imagine how the tongues would wag."

"You are weeping," he observed without looking down at her.

How did he know?

She sniffed. "Of course I am not. Do not be silly."

"I am a great many things, but I do not count silly amongst them." His tone was grim as he shouldered his way into a door and through the dimly lit halls of what was presumably his home. "You are in pain, and I have no wish to see you suffer. Even if your injury was caused by your own stupidity."

She frowned at him. "I nearly thought you a caring man, but that last sentence quite ruined the illusion."

A muscle in his jaw twitched. "Excellent."

He had brought them to a set of stairs which was lit with wall-hung sconces, and then began ascending.

"Put me down," she told him. "I am capable of walking."

"I trust you more when you are in my arms," he quipped. "You are less capable of causing me trouble."

Indeed. From her perspective, it was the opposite instead.

"My pain was momentary and it is gone now. Truly, think of what will happen should one of your servants come upon us," she hissed.

Although the prospect did not bother her in the slightest, she was suddenly desperate to be on her own feet and away from his warmth and delicious scent.

"This hall is private thanks to the diabolical proclivities of one of my predecessors," he intoned, reaching a landing and turning to ascend another flight. "Apparently, it pleased him greatly to bed his paramours in the privacy of his home and without the knowledge of his wife or servants."

"Ah, yes, far more civilized to bed one's paramour at a separate residence entirely," she said, and then scolded herself for the bitterness she could not seem to strip from her voice.

It should not matter to her that he had kept a mistress at the home where he had previously taken her. His past had no bearing on either her present or her future. And yet, she could not deny the burning coal of something that felt a lot like jealousy.

"Is that censure I detect in your voice, Miss Sutton?"

"I am merely pointing out the hypocrisy where I see it, milord."

She suppressed a shudder when he took them through a tight passageway that was decidedly dark and unlit. Her fingers dug into his shoulders and she pressed herself tightly against him as fear clawed up her throat.

It was irrational and she knew it, for it had been years since her father had left her locked in a tiny dirt-floored room as punishment, but that did not keep the old emotions at bay.

"You are going to leave marks, my dear."

Although his tone was easy, there was an unspoken question in his words.

One she did not want to answer. Although her oldest brother Jasper had done his best to protect Pen and her siblings from their father's wrath, he had been scarcely more than a lad himself.

A resurgence of memories better left buried along with her father sent fear shooting through Pen. She buried her face in the viscount's throat, despite her every intention to present herself as invulnerable.

"What is the matter, Pen?" he asked softly, still guiding them through the inky corridor, his footfalls steady and his breath scarcely labored.

She swallowed, trying to form an answer. "Nothing."

"Your ankle?"

"The ankle is fine," she denied.

"What, then?"

His persistence distracted her from the uncomfortable sensations buffeting her. But only for a moment as the darkness still surrounded them. She burrowed herself deeper into his neck, inhaling the familiar scent of him.

"Pen," he urged. "Tell me."

As if she ought to unburden herself to a man who had repeatedly told her he distrusted her and who was currently holding her captive at his town house. It hardly mattered. She could not manage a word past the fear clogging her throat. All she could do was keep her face pressed tightly to his neck, eyes shut against the darkness. Somehow, pretending the world around her was not enrobed in blackness helped to calm her madly racing heart.

There was a click as the viscount leveraged his body against something, followed by a slight creak.

"Here we are," he said, his voice a pleasant rumble against her ear.

She could feel the vibration of his baritone in his throat. But she was not prepared to look. "Where?"

"My chamber."

He had brought her to his chamber? The revelation left her so shocked that she tipped her head back, eyes opening, to find a room thankfully bathed in light. It was smaller than she would have expected for a viscount, but she could only suppose the chambers in the ducal apartments where the duke and duchess resided would have been suitably impressive. As it was, this room was far larger than any of the private chambers at The Sinner's Palace, and far more refined.

The furious panic that had rendered her almost helpless gradually ebbed, replaced by the rational part of her mind.

"Are you mad?" she demanded.

"Quite possibly." His response was calm, as if he had not just carried her from the mews through a secret passageway to the room where he slept, and as if she were visiting of her own volition rather than against her will. "After all that has recently come to pass, I expect so."

She shifted in his arms, more than aware of the manner in which their bodies were pressed together and terribly aware of the fact that her weight must be a leaden burden. "Put me down, Garrick."

Yes, she was using his Christian name once more. And why not? What better time to revert to familiarity with a gentleman than when she was in his bed chamber?

"You are certain your ankle is no longer paining you?" He frowned down at her, and whether it was reluctance to believe her or to let her go etched on his countenance, she could not say.

The weakest part of her most definitely knew which she would have preferred. But she had not come this far to play the fool to a viscount who would never love her or view her as his equal. She was a Sutton, curse it, and while she had been foolishly unarmed for her misadventures this evening, just as in other matters, she would make certain never to make the same mistake twice.

"It was a momentary pain, nothing more," she reassured him.

He lowered her to the sumptuous carpet. She bit her inner lip to keep from wincing as her ankle made a liar of her. She had certainly suffered worse, but it still ached with a dogged persistence that increased as she put her weight on it. Not that she would allow him to know. And why should he care, anyway?

His shrewd, ice-blue gaze was assessing. "Why were you trembling when I carried you through the corridor?"

Had she been? She refused to believe it. "I do not tremble. I'm a Sutton."

"You were shaking in my arms and clinging to me like a frightened cat."

She frowned. "What would you even know of cats, Lordly?"

He flashed her a tight smile. "Perhaps a bit, considering I keep one as a companion."

As if to punctuate his words, a small mewl interrupted their heated exchange.

Pen glanced down to find a fat chintz cat emerging from beneath a table, tail raised at an angle that suggested she was less than pleased. Green-gold feline eyes stared at her, and that easily, all the trepidation that had been daunting her throughout their sudden journey through the dark fled.

She knelt, ignoring the sharp pain in her ankle, and extended a hand for the cat. "Come, sweet kitten," she crooned. "I shan't hurt you."

The chintz cat watched her, holding still as she assessed the probability of friend or foe. Pursing her lips, Pen made the sound that never failed to attract the cats she fed behind The Sinner's Palace. None of them had a home, and they were each wary and bedraggled, but she was determined to see them get something in their little bellies.

When the feline refused to come nearer, Pen turned to Garrick. "What is her name?"

"How do you know she is a she?" he asked instead of answering.

"Her coloring," Pen answered. "There are many strays in the rookeries, and the chintz cats are always mamas."

"Next you will tell me you tend to the strays." He quirked a brow, his expression impassive.

Ducal.

She held his stare. "I do."

There was a pause before he finally responded. "Rosebud."

Her lips twitched, but she managed to suppress her mirth. This evening had taken a decidedly strange turn. "Ah."

"My mother named her. She is my mother's cat." He removed the hat from his head and raked his fingers through his hair, looking uncharacteristically ill at ease. "She has a preference for me, and thus, here she finds herself, the duchess having grown tired of Rosie's caterwauling in my absence."

Rosie. The viscount had a cat, and he had even given her a sobriquet. What an interesting discovery. The icy lord was far more complex than she had initially supposed, and Rosebud was one more example of that. He was a protective brother, a stickler for propriety, the heir to a duke who was well-known for his impeccable reputation, manners, and fashion. Yet, he was also the man who had kissed her with such fiery passion. The man who had brought her such delirious pleasure.

"Hmm," Pen said noncommittally before turning her attention back to the feline. "Come, Rosie. You are a darling, aren't you? So lovely."

Apparently, Rosebud was far easier to win over than her master. The chintz cat sidled nearer, finally rubbing herself sinuously against Pen's shins. She ran her hand along Rosie's spine, pleased to find her fur sleek and soft. Quite unlike the stray, distrustful cats she tended and on occasion managed to touch before they scampered away.

The cat arched into her ministrations, a new sound emerging from her that was not quite a growl of displeasure, but rather…

"You are purring, aren't you, Rosie my sweet?" she asked the cat with no small amount of smug satisfaction.

Rosie's response was to flop to her back, presenting Pen with her mostly white, soft belly. Pen obliged, giving her a soft rub.

"Traitor."

The grumble overhead reminded Pen that she and her newfound friend had an audience. And judging from the tone of his voice and the harsh set to his jaw, a disapproving one.

"It would seem your cat enjoys my company," she told him, sending a grin in his direction.

Something shifted in his countenance. "If you are not my brother's betrothed, then what the devil *are* you to him?" he demanded.

Perhaps Lord Lordly was struggling with the attraction he felt for her. It would certainly serve him right. Although he had accused her of far worse misdeeds, he was the one who had been kissing the woman he believed to be his brother's betrothed at every turn. Even now, he had spirited her away, when there was no rational reason to do so and she had told the stubborn oaf that she had no intention of wedding Aidan and bringing shame to the hallowed Weir family or the Dukes of Dryden past, present, and future.

She had a moment to consider her response. It would have been within her right to mislead him. To tell him a Banbury story of a cock and a bull. She could easily invent any number of tales that would have him shuddering in horror. But such a victory would be hollow.

"I am his friend," she said simply.

"Friend," Garrick repeated, incredulous.

"Yes, his friend." She turned her attention back to Rosie, who had begun batting at Pen's hand, her sharp claws finding purchase. "Just as I am your friend, little minx," she addressed the cat in the voice she ordinarily reserved for small children, her nieces included. "And if I am your friend, you mustn't poke me with those claws of yours. It is most impolite."

"Most impolite."

She sighed and cast a glance over her shoulder at the viscount, which proved a mistake. He was looking down at her with so much intensity that a wave of longing hit her in the chest and nearly sent her sprawling.

"That's what I said, Lordly."

He shook his head, as if clearing it of some troubling thought with physical force. "Earlier, you called me Garrick."

"That was before I remembered you have taken me captive out of some blockheaded notion I am somehow to blame for whatever ill has befallen Aidan," she pointed out, rising to her feet and facing him. "Tell me, what is your plan for this evening? You have brought me to your town house, to your chamber. I have warned you that when my family discovers me missing, they will stop at nothing to find me, and yet you have insisted upon this farce. Where am I to sleep?"

"In my bed," he said.

And she was sure she must have misheard him.

"In your bed? Apologies, yournabs, but whatever happened between us earlier ain't going to be repeated."

He huffed out the most endearing irritated sigh she had ever heard, which was proof she was every bit as addle-pated as the viscount was.

"Of course it is not," he said stiffly. "What occurred earlier was…regrettable. As a gentleman of honor, I can assure you it shall never happen again."

And what a pity that was, even if his use of the word *regrettable* made her long to plant her fist in his perfectly straight, patrician nose.

"Very regrettable," she agreed. "If I'm meant to stay the night until you can pluck your head out of your arse, then I have some bad tidings for you, Lord Lordly."

His nostrils flared at her deliberately coarse words. "I will thank you not to speak in such vulgar fashion, madam."

"You'll be sleeping on the floor," she said, ignoring him. "Rosebud and I will be enjoying that fine bed of yours while we pay a call to the land of nod."

His lips tightened, but he did not argue. "I was going to suggest as much myself, Miss Sutton."

"Earlier, you called me Pen," she reminded him in an intentional echo of his words.

"Earlier, I was daft," he grumbled.

She could not suppress her grin. "You still are."

CHAPTER 9

Garrick woke in the earliest strains of dawn to abject regret and an ache in his back, which was entirely suiting, when he thought about it. After all, what kind of an idiot would bring an unwed, thoroughly inappropriate woman—poorly garbed as a man—into his home, in the midst of the night, and then give her his bed?

Him, that was who.

Thank Christ he had told his valet not to wait for him the night before. Winston would await Garrick's ringing for him, as was his customary habit for a shave, his morning ablutions, and dressing. But there would be no ringing of the bell pull for him with his unwanted guest still under foot.

Speaking of which, where the devil was Rosebud? Ordinarily, she slept curled at his feet, a purring warmth he found rather soothing, though he would never admit it aloud. He was just as fond of the bit of fur as she was of him, much to the dismay of his valet, who grumbled over the perpetual presence of chintz cat fur on Garrick's coats.

Suppressing a yawn and a grunt of pain at the knot centered in his lower back—his right arse cheek had fallen asleep, by God—Garrick rose to a sitting position and looked to the far end of the chamber where his bed loomed. Taunting him not just with its promise of comfort and warmth, but with its occupant.

Or rather, make that occupants. For there, curled beside Miss Pen Sutton's counterpane-swaddled form, lay none other than *his* cat.

"Traitor," he grumbled.

Rosebud's ears twitched.

How like a female to be concerned for her own comfort rather than sacrificing it for the sake of loyalty to the man who kept her warm and fed. But then, he could hardly paint Rosebud with the same brush as Veronica. She had thrown him over for the Duke of Rollingham, and he did not suppose she had ever truly cared about him. Rosebud, at least, loved him.

Or so he thought.

The form on the bed stirred.

And so did his cock. For the sight of her long, auburn locks fanning on his pillow was more erotic than he had imagined it would be. Naturally, he had imagined. All night long until he had finally fallen asleep in misery on the hard floor. Regardless of how sumptuous the carpets were, the floor was not a place he wished to sleep again.

Ever.

Pen sat up, stretching her arms high over her head. The movement sent the counterpane slipping to her waist. And lecherous, unrepentant rogue that he apparently was, Garrick could not keep his gaze from slipping to the tempting fullness of her breasts and the stiff peaks of her nipples prodding the cambric.

He knew the precise shade of those nipples. Knew how they felt, hard and puckered in his mouth. Knew the soft sounds of need she made when he sucked them. And he knew how tight her cunny was, clamping around his fingers when she spent.

Damnation.

This was no way to begin the day, with a cockstand he could not ameliorate and a cat who had defected to the enemy side.

He scowled. "You are indecent, Miss Sutton."

Beautiful, too. He had only previously risen in the morning to one woman in his bed, and that woman had slipped into his blood like a poison. He had vowed to never allow another to have such power over him again.

And aside from this inconvenient lust raging though him for one very wrong fortune hunting East End siren, he had lived his life above reproach ever since he had so foolishly lost his heart.

"You are every bit as rude in the morning as you are in the evening, Lord Lordly," Pen returned, her tone crisp.

Naturally, she did nothing to hide herself.

He wondered if she had removed her trousers. Lord in heaven, if her legs were bare beneath that damned coverlet…

No. You will cease all vein of thought concerning Pen Sutton's breasts, nipples, limbs, cunny, hair, mouth... Fuck.

What had she done to him? He scarcely ever used epithets or coarse speech. Not even in his own bloody thoughts. Until *she* had entered his life.

"I will leave the chamber so you might have some privacy to prepare yourself for the day," he said, irritated by the hoarseness of his voice and the hardness of his prick.

Flipping back the counterpane he had used in the night for his makeshift bed, he rose to his feet. A sharp twinge in his back had him inhaling.

To his dismay, she was at his side in an instant, bare legs peeping from beneath her white shirt in proof that she had indeed removed her trousers. He had a brief glimpse of creamy calves and dainty ankles before he jerked his furious gaze upward.

"What is amiss?" she asked.

He ground his molars against another stabbing pain as he attempted to put some proper distance between them. "My back is aching. How is your ankle?"

"My ankle is well enough. I did warn you not to carry me up all those stairs, did I not?" Clucking as if she were a governess who had just found her charge committing some mischievous deed, she moved.

A hint of her floral scent hit him, and curse him for a fool, but he inhaled quickly, wanting more, wanting to somehow trap it inside his lungs and keep it there. But that was stupid, every bit as stupid as Aidan's decisions were. Nonsensical. A scent could not be preserved; it was fleeting, much like the loyalties of a woman or a feline. And if he did not take care, he would land himself in the same manner of trouble his ne'er-do-well brother had.

"My back aches from sleeping on the floor all night," he snapped, irritated with himself for weaknesses he had long since thought cured. Apparently, some lessons were more difficult to learn than others.

"Whose fault is that?" she asked pertly. "I have a bed of my own awaiting me at The Sinner's Palace. I most certainly did not need you to take me prisoner—"

"You are hardly a prisoner, madam," he interrupted wryly, attempting to shift and stretch his tensed back muscles and wincing as new pain flared.

"—and hold me against my will, forcing me to spend the night in your town house," she continued, as if he had not spoken at all. "I do hope for your sake that my brothers have chosen to react rationally and reasonably to the note you sent telling them where I have gone. Because knowing them, they will be knocking down your door, planting your butler a facer, and racing up the stairs any moment to find me."

As if on cue, a soft rap sounded at the door.

It would seem the previous day was doomed to repeat itself. Only, this time he was wearing far more clothing even if she wasn't. His eyes slipped to her bare feet.

How was it that even those were beautiful? He had never thought to take note of such a serviceable part of the feminine anatomy before. But then, it was entirely possible that it was not her feet he found alluring, but the woman herself. She seemed to have cast a spell of idiocy over him.

Likely, the same one she had cast over Aidan.

"My lord?"

The voice of his butler in the hall tore Garrick from his thoughts.

He cleared his throat. "Yes, Perkins?"

"I must beg your forgiveness for the intrusion at this early hour. However, there are several…ruffians…who are awaiting you in the drawing room. They have threatened the footmen with bodily harm and refuse to leave."

"That would be them," Pen said with a laugh. "I warned you."

"Hush," he whispered.

If anyone below stairs learned that he had brought an unknown female to his chamber last night, he had no doubt tongues would wag. It would only be a matter of time before his ignominy reached Mother and the rest of polite society. And Lady Hester, too.

To his butler, he called, "I shall be down forthwith, Perkins. Thank you."

"I will speak to them," Pen told him quietly. "After I explain what has happened to Lord Aidan, I doubt they will attempt to do you any harm."

She doubted?

How comforting.

"Of course they will not do me any harm," he snapped with more confidence than he felt. "I am the son of a duke, and they are lowborn East End thieves."

It was the wrong thing to say.

Her eyes flashed with fire. "My brothers are not thieves!"

"Use a quieter voice, if you bloody please," he growled. "I have no wish for the entire household to know I have secreted the fortune hunter who was attempting to swindle my brother into marrying her into my chamber."

"You would not need to worry about that if you had not forced me to come here when I had no wish to do so."

Her chest was heaving in her outrage, and damn it, but those nipples of hers...

No. Stop this. You can control yourself. There are far more important matters to attend to than Pen Sutton's magnificent breasts.

Pity he could not think of one.

He shook his head. Finding his brother. The Suttons. Ransom and a potential drubbing. And what to do with the minx before him.

Kiss her.

Bed her.

Damn it.

"Nonetheless," he bit out, "I will thank you to dress while I face your brothers."

"I will dress and face them with you," she countered, ever the stubborn wench he had come to know and admire.

Admire?

He hadn't had anything to eat for dinner last night. Likely, he was famished. Starving. He did feel a trifle lightheaded. He needed breakfast. That was the only suitable explanation for such a wretched notion to cross his mind.

"Your presence here is a secret," he reminded her. "It is imperative it remain that way."

She cocked her head, considering him from head to toe in a flirtatious manner that had him going hot all over. "I don't know, Lordly. I've grown rather fond of that big ducal beak of yours. I'd hate to see one of my brothers make it crooked for the rest of your life."

Lordly.

There it was again, the mocking diminutive she had lately pinned upon him. A bastardization of his title was bad enough, let alone an abbreviation of one. She was attempting to rile him again, he did not doubt.

Therefore, to spite her, he endeavored to keep his expression impassive. "You may save your childish insults, Miss Sutton. I am perfectly aware my nose is not at all overly large."

How haughty he sounded, even to his own ears.

"Eh, don't be such an old toast," she said, waving her hand in an expansive gesture that was decidedly unladylike. "My brothers can likely help you with finding Aidan. You'll be wanting to stay on their good side. Trust me."

He had no idea what an old toast was, but he knew it could not be anything good.

"Trusting you is the last thing I will do," he told her coolly, watching as *his* beloved Rosebud leapt from *his* bed to curl lovingly around the bare ankles of the scandalous fortune hunter before him. "Have you forgotten that is the reason for your presence here?"

The corners of her lips turned down in a delectable pout. "My imprisonment, you mean."

The urge to kiss her was almost potent enough to bring him to his knees.

What would she do if he peeled that shirt from her body, carried her to the bed, and fucked her until noon?

No, he could not very well carry her, could he? Not with his back in its present state.

He frowned. "You are not my prisoner but my guest."

"Doubt your rattling cove believes that," she grumbled.

Garrick was lost. "Rattling cove?"

"Coachman," Miss Sutton supplied. "Saw you carrying me about, he did. If you think the poor cull ain't going to spill the scandal broth to everyone he knows, you're more foolish than I thought."

Her accent was slipping, he realized. Her speech had become a mixture of East End accent and London drawing room. Which meant, he suspected, that she was somehow distressed.

"I would trust Neave with my life," he said honestly. "He is a loyal retainer."

It was imperative a man be able to know four people in his life would not deceive him: his coachman, his butler, his valet, and his housekeeper. Everyone else—parents, siblings, wife or mistress, could betray or deceive him at any moment. It was truth that nearly all of them had, though he had yet to take a wife.

Lady Hester.

What would the sweet-tempered, angel of a woman think of him were she to see him now, lusting after a scantily clad female who was her social inferior in every way? And in his bed chamber?

As if to offer reproach, Rosebud meowed loudly.

"You'll want me at your side when you face Hart and Wolf, if that's who's come," Miss Sutton said, bending down to offer his traitorous feline a scratch atop her head. "And Lord help you if it's Jasper and Rafe, too. Distrust me on everything else, but believe me when I tell you that. My brothers are fearsome when they are protecting their own."

For a ridiculous moment, Garrick almost blurted that she

was his, not theirs. Christ, he needed to eat something. His mind was clearly even more addled than he had previously supposed.

As if prodded by the thought, his stomach growled.

"You'll be wanting something to eat, I expect," she said, not bothering to pretend she had not heard the sound as any lady would do. "Put an end to your protesting, Lordly. I'm coming along whether you like it or not."

"Very well," he reluctantly agreed, having grown tired of arguing with her and wanting her and seeing her bare limbs on display.

To say nothing of her greedy nipples poking through her shirt…

Stop this madness, Garrick. Cease it at once.

"At long last, he shows some sense," the vexing woman said to his cat in conspiratorial fashion.

He was not certain whether he should laugh or weep. She was talking to Rosebud, and the cursed feline was meowing as if in agreement.

"You will dress and return to the mews through the secret corridor," he directed her instead. "Come to the front door, and you will be received."

She straightened, a sudden pallor in her complexion, her lovely features drawn tight in a way he had never seen before. "Has it any windows to light the way?"

"Of course not, else it would not be a secret." He searched her countenance, understanding dawning. "You have a fear of the darkness."

At last, her odd behavior the night before made sense. There was no other explanation for the manner in which she had clutched him, pressing so near their beings had nearly merged as one, her fingernails digging so tightly into his shoulders that he was certain there would be marks if he bothered to look.

Her spine stiffened, chin tilting up in defiance. "I fear nothing."

"I will give you a brace of candles," he said, something within him softening. Melting just a bit. "Will that suffice?"

"I hardly need it."

Her voice was unconvincing. It was difficult to imagine Pen Sutton being fearful of anything, let alone something as insignificant as the dark. Yet, she had to be.

What had happened to her to make her fearful of a lack of light?

And why did the question make his heart feel tight as a knot in his chest?

"Will you not tell me?" he asked, knowing it was not entirely his right, and yet wanting to understand her.

She was silent for a moment, and he expected her to continue her denial.

"My father was a tosspot, and when we angered him, he punished us children by locking us in a small, dark room. Some of us were punished more often than others. It ain't the dark I fear. It's the memories."

"Christ, Pen." He did not know what else to say.

Words eluded him. The thought of her as a young girl, locked inside a dark room as punishment, was enough to send bile up his throat.

She shook her head, the bravado she ordinarily displayed replacing the fleeting hint of vulnerability. "I don't need your pity any more than I need your bleeding brace of candles."

He would allow her to cling to her pride for now.

"Nonetheless, you ought to take it," he said, striving for lightness. "No need to go about bumping into my walls."

"I suppose not." The hesitant smile she sent him—part gratitude, part something he could not define—hit him like a blow. "You truly ought to go before my brothers come looking for you. I will join you in scarcely any time at all."

He nodded, tearing his gaze from hers before moving—with care, in consideration of his aching back—to the brace of candles he had promised and lighting each flame.

THE URGE TO thieve Garrick's sweet cat had been strong. *Garrick?* What was she thinking, continuing to consider him in such intimate terms? Pen heaved a sigh and inwardly chastised herself as she waited for the return of the butler who had eyed her in most suspicious fashion before offering to see if his lordship was at home.

At home.

She had bitten her tongue to keep from saying she knew his lordship was at home because she had spent the night in his bed. That would have ended badly for Lord Lordly. And for reasons Pen did not care to consider or dissect, she felt a sense of responsibility where he was concerned. If he did not wish to be gossiped about, she would protect him from it. Even if it meant finding her way through a small secret passageway with nothing but a brace of candles.

Confined spaces made her anxious.

Not as panic-stricken as the dark.

As it was, she had managed to emerge from the corridor without screaming, freezing, or bursting into tears. She considered that a victory, although she had admittedly been spurred on by images of violent clashes between her brothers and Garrick. Blood spurting from his nose. Purple bruising mottling his eye. She did not think any of them would stab him.

Being sent to rot in the hulks should prove a suitable deterrent.

Should it not?

She tapped her boot in the marbled entry hall, growing

impatient. Why was she waiting here, wasting her time, when she could be within, making certain her brothers were not pummeling poor Garrick with their fists?

The butler returned, his expression as grave as ever. "His lordship will see you, Mr. Sutton."

She hadn't a card, for her trips to bare-knuckle bouts and her other adventures about London with Aidan had most definitely never been the proper sort. She had never needed one. The lack had caused the butler's brow to wrinkle, and likely had been the source of her continued wait.

Pen followed the servant to what was presumably the drawing room, where her brothers and Garrick were within. The butler stood on the threshold, obscuring her view, and announced her in grim tones.

"Mr. Logan Sutton, my lord."

Sadness trickled through Pen at hearing her brother's name spoken aloud. How she wished it were Loge being presented to the drawing room now instead of herself. But he was long since gone to Rothisbones, having disappeared without a trace, leaving the rest of the family to carry on with heavy hearts.

The butler stepped to the side, and finally, after what seemed a lifetime of attempting to restore herself to a semblance of dress, forcing her way through the secret passage, and then arriving at the front door, she was officially paying a call upon Viscount Lindsey.

A man who was very much a stranger to her in some ways.

And a man who was very much *not* a stranger to her in others.

He was on his feet, looking every bit the distinguished lord despite the fact that he was dressed in day-old clothes. No one else would look upon him and know. She, however, did. Because she had spent the night in his chamber.

Their gazes met and held. For a moment, her heart ceased to beat, and then she recalled she was meant to be a gentleman.

She crossed the threshold, belatedly catching sight of her brothers. Hart and Wolf, thankfully. Jasper and Rafe were blessedly absent. Neither of her siblings appeared particularly pleased to see her, however.

Indeed, Wolf looked rather...deadly.

Oh dear.

"Mr. Sutton."

Garrick's voice tore her from her thoughts, and she bowed, keenly aware of the butler's presence at her back.

"Thank you, that will be all, Perkins," Garrick added, addressing the august servant behind her.

The drawing room door closed.

And pandemonium descended.

Hart and Wolf began shouting at once.

"I ought to skin you alive for what you've done."

"You'll be paying for taking our sister captive, you bleeding arsehole."

She swallowed hard. Oh dear, indeed.

"Wolf, you aren't going to skin anyone," she hastened to say, wondering if he had brought his knives. He did possess a rather menacing collection... "And Hart, Lord Lindsey did not take me captive."

Well, in truth, he had. Somewhat. If she had feared him, she would have fought and clawed and done everything in her power to escape him. But while he was a man who could enrage her, Garrick would never hurt her. She knew that much instinctively. No, she had known she was safe with him. He had browbeaten her into accompanying him, but a wicked part of her had not minded, regardless of how much of a fuss she had caused.

"Then how the bloody 'ell do you explain your disappearance last night?" Wolf demanded, scowling. "We didn't receive the note hisnabs sent us until dawn when we closed the club, or we would have been here with torches in hand, ready to burn this damned house to ash."

Wolf was furious. She had never before seen him this irate.

But just as she was about to offer further explanation, Garrick moved between herself and her angry brothers, apparently having no notion of the danger he faced. Wolf and Hart were beloved to her, but she would not wish their rage upon her most vile enemy.

"I will thank you to stop yelling at Miss Sutton, gentleman," he said coolly. "She has done nothing to warrant your ire. I would also strongly advise against any attempts at committing arson or skinning me alive."

His calm drawl would have made Pen laugh on any other day. But she was not certain what her brothers would do.

"Or you'll do what, Lindsey?" Wolf demanded, his lip curling. "You may be a lord but don't think that's enough to keep you safe."

"I'll ask you again," Hart added, "what the devil are you doing with our sister?"

Well, there were certainly some answers Garrick could give that Wolf and Hart would dislike mightily.

She sidestepped the viscount, who had been blocking her view of her siblings. Wolf and Hart were pacing the fancy drawing room like caged lions. It was just as she had feared, and she could not help but to wonder how their meeting had fared before her arrival.

"Lower your swords, all of you," she said. "Lord Lindsey asked for my help in finding his brother. Lord Aidan has gone missing, and his lordship received a demand for ransom suggesting he's being held by someone against his will."

He had not precisely asked. She very much doubted the viscount ever asked permission for anything. But that was neither here nor there.

"We've been telling you Lord Aidan Weir was trouble from the moment he first started sniffing your skirts," Wolf said flatly. "If he's been taken, it would serve 'im right."

"Don't pay the ransom," Hart advised. "You'll be better off."

Pen scowled at her brothers. "You are being terribly rude."

Wolf's eyes narrowed. "Why are you dressed as a nob and pretending to be Loge?"

"I was looking for Aidan as well," she admitted.

"We were looking together," Garrick said calmly. "If either of you has information concerning my brother, it would be greatly appreciated."

"Why don't you take the matter to the charleys, milord?"

"The ransom letter warned not to." The weariness in his voice was not lost on her. "As unbelievable as it may seem, I am unaccustomed to my family members being held against their will by unknown villains."

"None of that explains what 'appened last night," Wolf pointed out. "You were alone with hisnabs here, were you not, Pen?"

She tried not to think about what had happened between herself and Garrick the night before for fear her brothers would spy the flush in her cheeks. "Not alone."

Also, she was not telling a lie because they had not been alone in his chamber. Rosie had been there with them.

"Yet you spent the night here," Hart persisted.

"Yes," she said defiantly. "With no one for company save a cat. Now, do either of you know about anything suspicious happening at The Beggar's Purse? That is where Garrick is meant to deliver the ransom for Aidan."

The moment Hart's brow lifted, Pen cursed herself for her blunder. "Garrick, is it? Awfully familiar, Pen."

"Miss Sutton's honor is safe," Garrick said, his tone frosty. "You can rest assured I would not dream of sullying her."

"Something ain't right," Wolf declared. "But we've a gaming hell to run, and we can't afford to waste more time on a ne'er-do-well lord who has disappeared on his own. Pen, you'll be coming with us."

That was rather highhanded of him.

"You cannot tell me what to do, Wolf."

"Maybe not, but you ain't staying here," Hart said grimly.

"Of course not," she agreed. "However, we ought to accompany his lordship to The Beggar's Purse this evening. If Aidan is indeed being held against his will, he could be in danger. Lord Lindsey may need our aid."

And who better to offer protection than the Sutton clan, who were as feared as they were revered in the East End? They were not afraid to fight with their fists or any other weapons available to them.

Wolf shook his head slowly, pinning Garrick with a narrow-eyed glare. "I don't think you or your troublesome cove of a brother deserve our aid. Nothing but problems from the two of you, leading Pen on a merry chase around London dressed as a nob. Suttons protect our own, unlike the quality."

Garrick stiffened at her side. "Who are you to judge? You are fortunate I have yet to have you bodily removed from my drawing room after all the threats you and your brother have made against me and the insults you have paid your sister."

He was…championing her?

Pen turned to him with a burst of surprise, for she had not thought either of her brothers *had* insulted her.

"We've done nothing of the sort," Hart argued.

He inclined his head. "By suggesting she is untrustworthy,

you have."

She bit her lip to keep from reminding Garrick he had paid her the same insult. Repeatedly. That would most definitely not earn him any favor with Hart and Wolf, and she was very much attempting to keep the situation from devolving into a bout of fisticuffs or…worse.

"They meant to protect me," she hastened to add before either of her brothers could say something to further inflame the viscount's ire. "Please, if the three of you would simply calm yourselves, you would see that no harm has befallen me, no insults have been intended, no threats shall be carried out, and we can work together to make certain Aidan is returned safely home."

In the wake of her outburst, the silence was almost deafening. She waited as three sets of stony male gazes settled on her. Two hazel, one brilliant blue.

Garrick was first to speak. "The three of you are welcome to join me for breakfast. We can continue this discussion over some sustenance."

His stomach grumbled again, but she doubted Hart and Wolf could hear.

He had invited them to share a meal with him. It was a small olive branch, but she was willing to seize it with both hands. And her brothers were likewise not known to deny any offers of food.

With a wary expression, Wolf nodded.

"Aye," Hart said, "we'll eat your belly timber, viscount. And you'll tell us everything you know."

Wolf snorted. "Shouldn't take long."

"Twice as long as it would take you, Sutton," Garrick quipped, seemingly unaffected.

And not for the first time, it occurred to Pen that there were far more facets to the handsome viscount than she had previously supposed.

CHAPTER 10

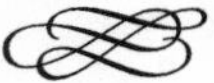

Breaking his fast had done nothing to aid the disturbing state of Garrick's mind. Nor had any of the subsequent meals he had taken. Apparently, what ailed him—the worm that had managed to infiltrate his brain and leave it addled—was not caused by hunger. There was no surer proof of that than the tableau in which he currently found himself. Namely, seated at a table at The Beggar's Purse in the armpit of the East End, surrounded by *Suttons,* of all people.

One of whom was not at all the gentleman she pretended to be. Rather, she was a beautiful, glorious auburn-haired siren he could not seem to cease thinking about. Or touching. Or kissing. Or lusting after. *Christ,* he wanted her more with every passing second of each cursed hour.

Yes, this was proof. As was his trust in the very people he had been so recently persuaded were his enemy. Whilst he had once deemed them fortune-hunting villains determined to manipulate and force their way into the upper echelon of polite society, Garrick had been forced to swallow his pride and revise his hastily formed opinions. Like Pen, her siblings were brash and bold, but they seemed…genuine. Dare he say it? Trustworthy.

He shifted on the uncomfortable bench that was biting so tenaciously into his arse and sipped at his ale, which was not nearly as bitter and terrible as he had expected it to be, given the dreadful state of the establishment. They were surrounded by the lowest of the low, wenches with their breasts nearly falling from their bodices as they sat upon the laps of roués whose hands were up their skirts. Some dangerous-looking fellows who appeared as if they would as soon look at a man as stab him in the gut.

Perhaps this had been a bad idea.

"You are certain you are familiar with the owner of this…" He paused, searching for a word to describe the sticky-floored hovel in which he found himself. "This *establishment*, Suttons, and that he will aid us?"

"She will," Wolf Sutton said, flashing the grin of a true rogue if Garrick had ever seen one. "She's a widow, and the lady and I are reasonably well acquainted."

The added qualification went a long way toward explaining the connection between the Sutton brothers and the proprietress. *Reasonably well acquainted* was likely the politest fashion in which Wolf Sutton had ever declared he had bedded a woman, too. Garrick could not be certain if he made the effort in deference to his sister's presence at the table or his own.

It did not matter. What did matter was that they were going to find Aidan and bring him home.

Tonight.

And then…

And then, Garrick would have no reason to ever spend another moment in Penelope Sutton's intoxicating presence.

Which was just as well, because he needed to concern himself with courting the woman he intended to wed instead of chasing a trousers-wearing hoyden across London.

Why, then, did the realization fill his chest with a hollow sadness?

He took a lengthy draught of his ale to chase the feelings away. Followed by another.

"This should all unfold relatively smoothly," said Hart Sutton, who was not nearly as brutish as his brother, the aptly named Wolf, was.

As far as Garrick could discern, Hart Sutton was the leader of the two, whilst Wolf Sutton was the brawn. Their roles were of little import to him as long as they helped him to secure his brother's safety, however.

"Does the proprietress believe the criminals in question are lodging in a room here?" Garrick asked Wolf Sutton.

A small part of his mind—the cynical portion that had its origins in Veronica's betrayal—cast up a reminder that it was possible they were all thick as thieves with the villains who had taken Aidan prisoner. Pen included.

However, another part of him refused to believe it. Rosebud trusted her, and Rosie had always been an excellent judge of character. She had hissed at Veronica on the few occasions when their paths had crossed.

"A woman has taken rooms," Wolf answered, before sipping his own ale and scowling. "Watered-down piss. I thought Elizabeth gave a damn about the quality she serves her patrons."

And here Garrick had deemed it not terrible. But then, he had never preferred ale. It was far too pedestrian.

"A woman," he repeated, turning this news about in his mind to make sense of it. "Why would she suspect a lone woman?"

"Apparently, she appeared with a nob, with just enough coin for the night. Then, a different cove paid the next evening's stay," Wolf explained, "and the same cove paid for the next."

Garrick found himself struck by an unexpected surge of gratitude. Regardless of their roughness about the edges, Pen and her brothers were proving damned helpful. He was not uniquely suited to the vagaries of dealing with criminals, swindlers, and East End riffraff. Navigating a drawing room, handling a phaeton, performing a country reel, offering a dowager lemonade, these were feats he could manage with ease. Rescuing his idiot brother from the maws of danger? Not so much.

"You are assuming the nob was my brother?" Garrick asked, trying to follow the logic.

In his world, a woman would never take rooms above a tavern on her own, and most definitely not with two different men. But then, The Beggar's Purse was about as far from his world as he could manage to find himself.

"Aye, that's the way of it," Wolf Sutton agreed, sounding reluctantly impressed. "You aren't as thick-witted between the ears as you look."

Coming from most men in Garrick's acquaintance, such words would have been cause for pistols at dawn. However, he recognized the grudging admiration in the other man's gruff tone. It would seem the Suttons were all eccentric in their own ways. How vexing to discover he did not despise them as he ought.

He raised his ale in mock salute. "A compliment from you, no doubt, sir."

"Forgive Wolf," Pen said, drawing Garrick's attention. "His tongue works faster than his mind."

"The ladies haven't complained yet," Wolf said with a grin.

Garrick, who had been in the process of taking another sip of ale to calm the rampant desire that seemed to afflict him whenever Pen was near—and even when she was not, for that matter—subsequently choked on his beverage, inhaling some of it.

Hart Sutton pounded on his back with more force than necessary. Garrick hastily swallowed and attempted to regain his composure. Not an easy task when the other man was continuing his dubious ministrations. A strong arm on Hart Sutton, that was certain. Garrick rather suspected the man was attempting to get even with him for the slights he believed Garrick had paid Pen the night before.

And, well, he was not wrong. Whilst nothing untoward had occurred at his town house, if Hart and Wolf Sutton were privy to what had happened on that French sofa on the other side of town, they would not be seated with him at this table in civilized fashion. He had no doubt they would be tempted to tie weights to his ankles and toss him into the Thames. He could not fault them.

What he had done with Pen the night before was unconscionable. Not only because she was an unmarried woman, and she was wholly inappropriate for him as a match, but also because he intended to marry another. Lady Hester would never accept his suit if she knew the truth, that he had been pleasuring an East End hoyden when he was meant to have been courting her at some mind-melting musicale.

"I believe you have thumped his lordship's back enough," Pen said in Garrick's defense.

Bless her, but her words only heightened his blistering inner shame. It was not merely Rosebud's approval that had altered the light in which he viewed Miss Sutton. Rather, it was the woman herself.

"He's still sputtering, Pen," Hart said, continuing his blows, sounding rather pleased with himself.

And so he was, but the other man's supposed attempts at aid were doing nothing to help the matter.

He moved his chair nearer to Pen's, beyond her brother's reach. "Thank you, Sutton. That is quite enough, I assure you."

Pen's knee bumped into Garrick's beneath the table, and he had to suppress a groan and a corresponding surge of need. Her sweetly floral scent reached his nostrils, a welcome alternative to sour ale, smoke, and sweat that seemed to be the foremost odors in The Beggar's Purse.

It took every bit of restraint he possessed to keep from reaching beneath the table and placing his hand on her inner thigh, caressing higher to the apex of her legs where he knew he would find her hot and silken and, if the world were fair, decadently wet.

Aidan, he reminded himself. *You have come here to bring your brother back to the loving bosom of his family and not to seduce the woman at your side.*

"That was unspeakably rude of you, Wolf," Pen chastised her brother. "Poor Lord Lindsey nearly choked on his ale. You owe him an apology."

Wolf Sutton smirked, nary a hint of remorse in his countenance. "Forgive me, milord. For a moment there, I forgot we had left our family's hell in the care of others to come here and chase after your no-account brother who managed to get himself kidnapped by a filching mort."

The sarcasm was not lost on Garrick, even if he was uncertain what a *filching mort* was. A lady thief?

He cleared his throat, his breathing restored to its customary rhythm at last. "I do appreciate the favor you and your siblings are paying myself and my family, Sutton. As I said this morning, it shall not go unrewarded."

"We do not require a reward for doing what is right," Pen inserted stubbornly. "Is that not the way of it, brothers?"

"A small reward would not be entirely—bleeding hell, that hurt, Pen," said Hart Sutton, casting a scowl in his sister's direction. "I'll take those boots from you if you don't stop using them to kick my damned shins."

"We do not require a reward," she repeated pointedly, unconcerned by her brother's threat concerning her footwear.

Garrick had to admit that the sight of her in boots and trousers was rather growing on him. Seeing her lush curves on display for anyone else, however, was another matter. He had caught more than one roving eye on her finely formed limbs as they had entered The Beggar's Purse earlier. He had no doubt that no one was fooled; even a man who had lost his sight would know Pen Sutton was a woman.

And a glorious one at that.

But that thought, like so many others, was distinctly unwelcome at the moment.

He consulted his pocket watch and discovered the appointed time was nigh. "It would seem we have reached the pinnacle of this particular drama. I shall leave the one thousand pounds at the rear as the missive suggested."

Garrick was aware of Pen's gaze on him, it was searing, rather like a touch. He turned to her.

"Tell me you did not bring one thousand pounds," she told him with a wince.

"Of course I did."

If he had to pay the blunt to whomever was behind this, he would. As long as it meant Aidan was freed.

"Christ, Viscount. That was bleeding stupid," Wolf Sutton added with a chortle.

"We oughtn't be surprised," Hart Sutton said to his brother.

"Lads," Pen snapped. "You are not helping matters one

whit." She turned back to Garrick. "The charleys The Sinner's Palace keeps on retainer are on duty this evening, and we've asked them to surround The Beggar's Purse. You'll not need to pay a scrope to free Aidan."

He nodded, because it was the most efficient response. No need to argue or belabor the point any further. He had brought the coin, and he was willing to pay. He had learned from Veronica that a man should trust no one. Not even a woman who professed to love him with all her heart.

Especially not then.

"I will do as we planned," he said, before rising from the table.

"Do you want me to accompany you?" Pen asked.

"You ain't going with his lordship," Wolf Sutton growled.

"You'll be staying here," Hart Sutton said.

Apparently, her brothers did not know her at all. For if there was anything that guaranteed Pen was going to do something, it was to offer her opposition. Her pride would not allow it.

She was on her feet before he could blink, pinning her brothers with a determined stare. "I will be accompanying his lordship, and that is final."

The Sutton brothers exchanged a glance before the eldest shrugged and turned back to her.

"Suit yourself," he said, "but if anything goes awry, you'll be the one facing Jasper's wrath, not us."

"I will," she said with a nod.

Garrick wondered who the devil Jasper was, jealousy bolting through him like a runaway colt. But he tamped it down, telling himself it was likely another brother. And even if it was a lover, what should it mean to him?

Only everything.

He banished the unwanted thought.

"I will protect Miss Sutton with my life," he vowed to her brothers. "I am an expert marksman."

To that end, he had a pistol secreted in his coat, and he would not hesitate to use it if necessary. He may be a gentleman, but he was not a complete and utter noddy. The Suttons appeared unimpressed, however, despite his words.

"Come," Pen said with a nod of her head toward the rear of the establishment. "'Tis the alley where you must meet them, no?"

Apparently, she had been beneath this roof before and knew her way around the establishment. Likely, with Aidan. Yet another stab of jealousy hit him. He did not like the thought of her doing anything alone with his brother, even if they truly were friends as she claimed.

But he followed her, just the same.

They made their way through the throng of raucous men and women, through smoke and laughter and an endless number of unseemly displays. Christ, his mother would be horrified if she knew he had ever entered such a place, let alone spent so much time in the company of a woman who knew her way around one.

At last, they reached the darkened street behind The Beggar's Purse, where he had been instructed to leave the ransom at half past ten. It occurred to him that the missive had not been specific. He searched through the murky shadows in an effort to find a proper place where he might be expected to leave the funds. But when he reached into his coat to extract the notes, Pen's hand seized his wrist.

He would be lying if he said that touch did not move him.

"What are you doing?" he demanded curtly.

"Hush," she whispered. "There is someone else here, watching us."

How she could see anything through the inky darkness, he could not say. Garrick's eyes had yet to adjust, and he doubted they would. He could do nothing but accept her word.

Trust her.

Did he dare, truly and fully? Completely? He should not.

"Where is your pistol?" she asked next.

But then her hand was within his jacket, fingers searching, seeking, finding its hiding place unerringly. He was so affected by her touch that he reacted far too slowly.

"Blast it, Pen," he growled. "Give me that."

"No," she said simply.

His mind went wild with possibilities. Did she even know how to properly handle a pistol? Was she intending to rob him? Shoot him? Had this entire melodrama been a farce authored by her? Why the devil had her brothers decided to stay within, and where were the damned watchmen the Suttons had promised?

"Stop where you are," Pen said in a low voice filled with calm authority.

Through the shadows, he could discern the shape of her, the pistol in her hands, pointed at something in the distance. The hair on the back of his neck stood on end as an eerie shiver rolled down his spine. There was a scraping sound, then booted footfalls rushing forward, toward Pen.

"Give me the blunt and no one will get hurt," growled a low, masculine voice. "If you don't do as I say, I'll shoot."

Without thought, Garrick threw himself forward, determined to keep Pen from harm. His body slammed into another with so much force, his teeth clacked together. But Garrick had been spending a great deal of time at Winter's Boxing Academy recently, and he was more than prepared. Spurred on by the thought of any harm coming to Pen, he slammed his fist into the face of his shadowy opponent and was rewarded by the crunch of bone.

Hopefully he had broken the villain's nose. But Garrick

was not prepared to stop there. He had to make certain Pen was safe. The need to protect Pen driving him, he delivered punches to his opponent's jaw and midsection.

Garrick's fists flew with increased assurance, landing blows wherever he could. The man grunted, attempting to swing back, but Garrick had the advantage and overpowered him until his foe was on his back in the seedy alley, pinned by Garrick's knee on his chest.

His heart was thundering in his ears, victory roaring through his veins.

"Stop! Please! Christ in heaven, stop, you madman!" begged his opponent. "I surrender."

"Garrick!" Pen's worried voice cut through the haze of bloodlust surrounding him. "Are you hurt?"

Whilst the other man had landed some blows, he was teeming with so much fury that he scarcely felt a thing.

"I am well," he managed. "What of you?"

"I am unhurt as well."

Thank God. If anything had happened to her...no, he could not bear to think of such a terrible possibility.

The man beneath him moaned with pain, jolting him back to the present.

"Where is Lord Aidan Weir?" Garrick demanded of him.

Just then, a pair of watchmen dashed down the alley, carrying lanterns that chased the darkness.

"I'll take you to him," the man said.

In a small, threadbare chamber above The Beggar's Purse, Aidan was tied to the headboard of a narrow bed, a faded coverlet at his waist scarcely preserving his modesty. From what Pen could tell as she peered over Garrick's shoulder, he appeared to be entirely unclothed. Nary a stitch on him.

She had been prepared for any number of sights. But strangely, this had not been one of them. She found herself newly relieved the watch had taken away the man Garrick had defended her against in the alley, along with his wife, who had been found awaiting her husband in a hired hack near the front façade of The Beggar's Purse. The plan had been for the two of them to abscond with the one thousand pounds, leaving poor Aidan in his current state.

Hart and Wolf were awaiting them below, Wolf taking the opportunity to charm the proprietress and give her his opinion on the state of her ale. Pen had offered to accompany Garrick, needing to know for certain that her friend was safe as the man and his wife had claimed.

"Garrick," Aidan greeted his brother, relief in his voice, "thank Christ. I need to piss. Untie me, will you?"

Pen laughed, but after the unexpected upheaval of the last half hour, first with the assailant rushing them in the alley and then with the frantic race upstairs to find Aidan, the sound emerged as somewhat hysterical.

"That is the manner of greeting I receive?" Garrick snapped coolly. "After Miss Sutton and I were nearly attacked as we tried to pay the ransom to save your miserable hide?"

"Pen?"

At the sound of her friend's voice, she dutifully stepped to the side, revealing her presence. Aidan's eyes were wide as they met hers, and his mouth opened, then closed, as if he was searching for the proper words and failing miserably. "What the devil are you doing here?"

A flush darkened his cheekbones, presumably at being caught *en flagrante delicto* after what she could only suppose was a tryst gone wrong with the woman who had lured him to The Beggar's Purse.

"Lord Lindsey enlisted my brothers and me to help find you and secure your freedom," she said grimly.

"Here now," Aidan said, casting a glance toward the viscount, "who gave you leave to squire my betrothed about the East End?"

Garrick was holding himself stiffly at her side, his posture exuding anger. "Miss Sutton is not your betrothed, and you know it. You ought to be wailing with endless gratitude for my coming to your rescue instead of chastising me."

"Oh, Aidan," she said with a sigh, shaking her head. "What manner of scrape did you land yourself in this time?"

He cast a wry glance to his bound wrists. "That should rather be apparent, should it not? Untie me, let me find a chamber pot, and I'll tell you everything."

"You dare to laugh?" Garrick stepped forward, striding for the bed. "How could you, after what you have put us all through? I ought to box your damned ears. Miss Sutton might have been hurt or worse in that alley."

Aidan had the grace to look shamefaced. "I was drunk as David's sow, celebrating my impending nuptials, when Mrs. Knightly offered her companionship for the evening."

Of course Aidan would have been celebrating that ridiculous false betrothal he had dreamed up. And only he would have been celebrating with another woman. Pen would have said it served him right, but she did hate to think of what he must have endured the past few days.

"Fine husband you would make," Garrick muttered. "Carousing with lightskirts to celebrate your betrothal."

"I was celebrating Father's outrage more than anything else," Aidan confided, wincing as he tugged at his wrists. "Make haste, will you? I've been waiting for Mrs. Knightly to return for hours, and I'm not going to last much longer."

He was referring to his need to relieve himself. Mortification made her cheeks go hot.

"You are a treasure, brother," Garrick said, his voice frigid. "A true credit to the Weir family name."

He extracted a blade from his coat and began slicing at Aidan's bonds.

"I am sorry, Pen," Aidan said, looking back to her. "I never meant for this to happen. Will you forgive me? I swear to you that I will be a better husband."

"We are not going to be married," she said, amazed he apparently seemed to be taking the notion seriously, even after all that had come to pass. "I told you before you disappeared that I had no intention of wedding you, and despite your determination to utterly ignore my wishes, my opinion on the matter has not changed."

"I will earn your trust," he said. "I've made some realizations these last few days, and I treated you poorly. Allow me to make amends. Grant me another chance."

Surely he could not be serious.

Pen blinked, certain her eyes were deceiving her. But Aidan was still seated, bare-chested in the bed, eyes—so bright blue and like his brother's—entreating.

"You should go, Miss Sutton," Garrick said coldly before she could think of a sufficient response to offer.

Her gaze flew to him, finding his countenance all harsh angles and planes, curiously devoid of emotion. Once more the icy, arrogant lord. And she had been dismissed.

She nodded, for it was just as well that she take her leave. If Aidan was indeed bare-arsed naked beneath that coverlet, she had no wish to see the other half of him. He had always been like another brother to her, one to fill the hole in her heart left by Logan's abrupt disappearance.

"Of course," she said, doing her utmost to tamp down the ridiculous hurt rising within her at Garrick's abrupt shift in demeanor. "I will leave the two of you to privacy. Hart and

Wolf are likely still sorting out matters with the charleys and may need my assistance."

She turned on her heel and hastened to the door.

"Pen, wait," Aidan called after her.

But the one voice she truly wanted to hear asking her to come back remained silent. And why should she be surprised? Now that he finally had what he wanted—his brother restored to the family and no scandalous betrothal looming on the horizon—he had no further need of Pen. Likely, she would never see him again.

It was just as well, she told herself as the door clicked closed behind her. They belonged to different worlds, she and Lord Lordly. And like every other man in her life who was not one of her brothers, he had used her when it was convenient. Used her to gain what he wanted.

Now, he was tossing her aside. Just as Daniel had.

But although she knew it was for the best, she could not deny the ache in her heart as she descended the narrow stair to the public rooms below. Aidan was safe, the man and woman behind his kidnapping were in the custody of the charleys, and she could carry on with her life without the interference of one arrogant heir to a duke.

She was happy. Truly.

Her brothers were waiting for her when she reached the crowded, bustling tap-room.

"Pen," Hart said, frowning as she rejoined him and Wolf. "Where the bleeding hell have you been? We were about to come looking for you."

"I was making certain Lord Lindsey was reunited with Lord Aidan," she said, blinking away the sting of foolish, impending tears. "The Knightlys did not appear to do him any harm."

"Thank Christ," Wolf said, his tone dark. "We've wasted

enough bleeding time 'ere swilling watered-down ale and chasing after nobs."

"Yes," she agreed through a throat gone thick with unwanted emotion, "we most certainly have. We should get back to The Sinner's Palace where we are needed most."

And to the devil with everyone else.

Especially the brothers Weir.

CHAPTER 11

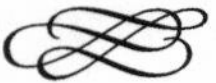

"Christ, this is a deuced depressing affair."

On any other day, the grumbling emerging from Garrick's side—Aidan, newly restored to the family flock and doing penance by pretending to be on his best behavior—would have given him cause to deliver a crushing quip. He would secure a lemonade and dance a lively quadrille and force his brother to charm some dowager or other. Indeed, on any other day, mingling with the cream of London society at Rivendale's would have been all he desired.

But this was not any other day. It was *today,* two full evenings after Garrick had last seen Pen Sutton. He could close his eyes till the day he died and still have the imprint of her swaying hips and lush bottom, scarcely hidden in her drab gentleman's garb, etched on the insides of his eyelids. Yes, he had dismissed her, the flash of hurt on her lovely face chipping away at a part of himself he had thought long withered and dead before she had summoned her pride and hidden it. Before she had *gone.*

He cleared his throat and forced himself to respond in the

fashion he would have before Pen Sutton had invaded his life. "There is nothing depressing about this dance. Half London would give their eye teeth to be here and you know it."

While it was true that vouchers for Rivendale's were an exclusive commodity everyone wanted and few could command, the knowledge somehow seemed to have lost its luster.

Because Pen Sutton had taken her leave from that shabby room above The Beggar's Purse two nights before, and he had not seen her since.

He had wanted her to go, of course.

He *needed* her to do so, he reminded himself sternly. Just as he needed to return to his life as it had been ever since he had devoted himself to becoming the next Duke of Dryden. Ever since Veronica's betrayal, which should have proven to him beyond question that a calm, unaffected society marriage was what he wanted. What was best. Mother and Father never argued. They were always perfectly pleasant to each other.

"Half London is bloody mad if you ask me," Aidan muttered.

He slanted a quelling look in his brother's direction. "No one asked you."

Aidan shifted from his right foot to his left, looking as ill at ease as Garrick felt. "I'm not meant for this twaddle, and you know it."

"Only look at Mother beaming upon you now," he said, with a surreptitious nod in the duchess's direction, on the other end of the ballroom.

She did indeed look pleased, the plumage in her turban fairly quivering with her delight at seeing her youngest son playing the role of proper gentleman at a soiree over which she reigned supreme as one of the *ton*'s most respected ladies.

Between them, young ladies and lords danced in perfect rhythm, nary a step out of time, as the most alluring debutantes sought to secure their future husbands.

"She looks at her cats in the same fashion," Aidan drawled, "and I'll be damned if she tries to feed me the gizzard of a fowl. Entrails of any sort make me bilious."

It was true that their mother had a tendency to care for her felines, whom she adored, more than she did her sons. At least, her outward expression of emotion seemed to suggest so. Lilac, Sweet Pea, and William were her crowning achievement, and most of her day—when she was not paying social calls or ruling Rivendale's—revolved around keeping company with her cats.

"I ought to feed you gizzard after the torment you unleashed upon us all, first with your supposed betrothal—"

"There was nothing supposed about it," Aidan interrupted hotly.

"—and then your drunken idiocy that led to you being kidnapped by a pair of thieves and held for ransom in some officious-smelling East End hovel," Garrick finished, taking a thorough look around him to make certain no sharp-eared gossips were within listening range.

Thankfully, they were not.

It would never do for word of what had befallen Aidan to travel. Mother would be humiliated. Aidan would be a laughingstock. Father could well succumb to his weak heart. And their other brother Jonathan, currently campaigning in the country, would see his aspirations as an MP dashed. The scandal would cause irreparable damage if the world discovered the youngest son of the Duke and Duchess of Dryden had been in his cups and celebrating his pending nuptials to an East End hoyden by bedding a lightskirt when he had been kidnapped and tied naked to a bed.

Humiliating did not begin to describe it.

"The Beggar's Purse is not entirely a hovel," Aidan said then, frowning mightily. "I will own that I have made some mistakes. Many mistakes. But I have had ample time to think about my actions, and there is one thing I have realized above all others."

Garrick's gaze caught on Lady Hester and her mama, hovering near to Mother's elbow. He owed her a dance. He also owed her a proposal. But his desire to offer either had been terribly diminished ever since a stubborn, auburn-haired minx had entered his life.

Do not think of her now. She is where she belongs, just as you are where you belong.

Pity those words no longer rang with the same truth he had once believed they did.

He jerked his attention back to Aidan, thinking Lady Hester could wait for another dance or two. Or three. Or ten. "Dare I ask what realization you reached? If it is not what an utter jackanapes you are for having invented your betrothal merely to hurt Mother and Father, only to disappear and cause me all manner of headaches as I sought to find you, I have no wish to hear it."

"I know I was wrong," Aidan said gravely. "I do not deny it, and I am sorry for any upset I caused. I was selfish and reckless, only concerned with what I wanted instead of what Pen wished. I will never forgive myself for that."

Pen.

The reminder that his brother had been close with her first rankled.

"You have the right of it," he forced himself to say, crushing any feelings of jealousy that attempted to rise to the surface. "You were indeed selfish and reckless, and you ought to be ashamed."

"So you have been telling me for the past two days."

He scowled at his brother. "Because you need to understand the ramifications of your actions."

"I do understand them," Aidan announced, his countenance brightening. "And that is why I know what I must do next."

Anything short of groveling would not be sufficient.

"And what is that?" he asked, curious in spite of himself.

"Beg Pen's forgiveness and ask her to marry me in truth."

Garrick nearly swallowed his own damned tongue. "Have you not learned your lesson?" he demanded, cursing himself for the loudness of his outburst, the sheer, raw reaction. He took a slow, deep breath, attempting to calm himself. "Look at me, Aidan. You have caused enough problems for Miss Sutton and for our family. The least you can do is to find a suitable young lady from a noble family, cease gadding about gambling and wenching and drinking yourself to perdition, and forget all about Miss Penelope Sutton."

And Garrick was going to do the same. The last bit, anyway. He was going to banish Pen from his thoughts, from his yearning, from his mind.

All he had to do was see her one last time, and then, he would bid her farewell forever. He did not know where the thought emerged from, but once it had appeared, it remained tenacious, refusing to be tamped down or otherwise chased away.

One more time. Yes. One more time, and he could say his goodbyes. That evening at The Beggar's Purse had been far too rushed and jumbled. His emotions had been overwhelming, and he had pushed her away in a reactionary way.

But after all the time they had spent together, surely a true goodbye was warranted. If he could meet with her again, speak with her, he was sure it would be the cure to what ailed him. A final severing of the ties that had bound them would render him free. Free to pursue Lady Hester with an unburdened conscience.

"I'll not do it," Aidan denied, stubborn and foolish as ever. "I can never forget about Pen. You have met her. You ought to know the impossibility of striking her from your mind. She is unique. An original."

Yes, she was. And yes, he did.

"You will have to," he countered. "Else, I will have no choice but to tell Mother and Father about where you have been and why. I do imagine Father would cut off your purse strings quite readily were he to learn the truth, do you not?"

Aidan paled, and Garrick knew a moment of guilt for his threat, necessary though it was. "You can do as you wish, Garrick. I need to do right by Pen, and I'll not stop until I do."

Garrick bit his inner lip. "Damn it, Aidan, you've done enough. Leave the lady be."

He ought to have been saying the same words to himself.

And yet, as he turned his gaze back toward Lady Hester on the opposite side of the assembly room, he knew he could not. He had to see Pen one more time.

Tonight.

THE HOUR WAS LATE, and after an exhausting evening spent working on the ledgers she had been neglecting over the last few days, Pen was drained. Her head ached, her eyes were strained, her fingers were cramped and ink-stained from so much tallying, and yet, the greatest pain afflicting her of all was not even physical in nature.

Rather, it was her heart. Her silly, fickle, ridiculous, foolish, utterly useless heart.

As she walked the familiar corridor in The Sinner's

Palace to her chamber door, the realization she had been avoiding since she had last seen Garrick hit her. She had fallen *in love.* Again. The heart she had believed broken, dashed to bits, and incapable of feeling after Daniel, had proven her wrong. For it now belonged to Garrick Weir, Viscount Lindsey, heir to a duke, proper, elegant, perfect aristocrat.

A man as out of reach to her as the stars and the moon and the sun.

She nearly staggered under the weight of the unwanted knowledge. Instead, she summoned her strength with a deep breath, and forced herself to continue the handful of steps to her door. A night's rest awaited. She would close her eyes and not see his face, but fall into the pleasant abyss of slumber instead. Go to a place where he could not haunt her every waking hour.

You are stronger than this, Penelope Sutton. You have already learned your lessons the hard way.

She would forget all about Garrick, just as he had forgotten her. Nary a word from him. Not even a curtly phrased missive thanking her and her brothers for the role they had played in helping to bring Aidan home and seeing his captors jailed. Not so much as a syllable since he had told her to go.

Why should she be surprised that the lofty lord—who loved to look down his nose at her whenever he was not kissing her senseless—had not returned to plague her? She ought not. He had been clear from the moment they had first met that he did not want her in his brother's life. Naturally, he would not want her in his either. She was the sort of woman a nob like him bedded but never wedded.

Which was perfectly fine with Pen. She never wanted to marry. Her life here at The Sinner's Palace was complete. She would dote on her oldest brother Jasper's daughters and any nieces and nephews which followed, keep the ledgers, and never again let an arrogant viscount's lips touch hers.

She opened the door to her chamber, and all her stern bravado fled.

For there, in the center of the small space that was purely her own, stood none other than Lord Lordly himself, just as handsome and forbidden as ever. How out of place he looked in his formal evening wear, dressed as if he were about to attend a fancy societal ball.

Because probably he either was or already had.

Her heart ached at the sight of him, so beloved and unwanted at the same time.

"My lord," she said, shocked.

He executed a perfect bow, flawless as ever. "Pen."

His familiarity was not lost on her. However, she would not pin her hopes upon a name. Likely, he had only found his way to her chamber that he might accuse her of more sins. Perhaps he was here to suggest yet again that she was somehow involved in the plot the Knightlys had devised to swindle Aidan's family out of one thousand pounds.

Grudgingly, she dipped into an abbreviated curtsy in return before rising, determined to learn why he had come.

"What are you doing here in my chamber?" she asked, casting a careful glance around her to make sure no one else was moving about in the corridor.

It would not do for any of her siblings to see him in her room, but she was also hesitant to cross the threshold and join him within. Being alone with him, and in proximity, seemed terribly reckless at the moment.

"Thank Christ it is yours." His solemnity broke as he flashed her a charming grin, the kind that reached his eyes. "I was not certain if I dared trust the scamp whose palm I greased to show me the way."

It was not the first time he had bought his way into the

private quarters of The Sinner's Palace. Heavens knew she should not be surprised he had done so again, though she and her siblings had given those in their employ a stern reprimand about allowing patrons to encroach on their sacred territory.

"I suppose a future duke's money can buy you all manner of things," she said bitterly, reminded of their disparate circumstances.

With Aidan, the differences between their worlds had never mattered. Yet with Garrick, it did, because she had allowed herself to fall for him, and he would never return those feelings.

"Not everything," he said, his gaze seeming to devour her face. "Not the things that matter most."

She wanted to ask him what he meant, but he had not answered her initial question, and if any of her brothers were to find him here, she shuddered to think what would happen. Although Wolf and Hart had been reluctantly understanding about that night at The Beggar's Purse and the evening before it, they remained disapproving of the quality in general and the Weir brothers in particular. They had been repeatedly warning her against future interaction with either of them. But in truth, there was only one Weir brother who made her heart pound faster and her knees go weak.

There was no help for it. She was going to have to join him in the room and close the door for the sake of their privacy. But that was fine. She could resist him. She was strong. She was a Sutton.

She stepped over the threshold and closed the door at her back. The action seemed to make the room one hundred times smaller and her skin a thousand times hotter.

Pen crossed her arms over her chest in a defensive gesture and reverted to humor in an attempt to distract herself from how badly she wanted to throw herself into his arms. "Well, Lord Lordly? What have you to say for yourself? What brings you to my lowly corner of the East End now? Perhaps you have decided I am torturing orphans or am plotting to kidnap your cat."

The thought of Rosie made a bittersweet pang in her heart, joining the ache. His adorable feline had been a surprise. She could not shake the impression there was far more to Garrick than she had initially supposed. But he was not hers to discover, and nor would he ever be.

"Nothing as insidious as that," he said calmly, his sinful lips still compressed in a stern slant, as if he wanted to smile but refused to allow it.

He took a few steps in her direction, bringing him nearer. Almost close enough to touch.

She remained at the door, watchful, not trusting herself in his presence. The time since she had seen him last had felt like a terrible eternity. "What, then?"

"You," he said. "You have brought me here, Pen. I had to see you."

The rawness of his voice, coupled with the admission itself, took her by surprise.

She was too ragged around the edges, too foolishly happy at his concession. Too pleased he was here, with her, even if the visit was to be fleeting. *Mine,* cried her heart. If only for tonight.

But still, she lingered where she was, two steps and a dreadful decision separating them. "Why did you have to see me?"

He moved again. One step. Two steps. Close enough to touch.

Oh Lord, he was tempting. His scent reached her, and those bright-blue eyes were fixed upon hers. She could not look away. How she had missed him.

"Because I did not properly convey my gratitude when

last I saw you." He shook his head, tucking an errant tendril of hair that had escaped her coiffure behind her ear. "You and your brothers were gracious to aid me in my efforts at finding my brother. It is a credit to you all that he was found unharmed and that not a single tongue has wagged with scandal broth. Your discretion is most appreciated."

She tipped her chin up. "You might have sent a note instead."

There hardly seemed a reason for him to come to her, to tempt her with what could never be hers.

"I might have done," he agreed, his hand still lingering at her face as he cupped her cheek.

He was not wearing gloves, and the caress of his bare skin over Pen's was enough to make a shower of sparks flit through her. Longing accompanied the fire. The need to touch him, to be touched by him.

"I am glad you did not," she confessed, heart pounding swiftly.

His thumb glided across her cheekbone. "Oh? And why is that?"

She wetted her suddenly dry lips. "Because a missive cannot kiss me."

He moved first, a low groan tearing from his throat, taking her into his arms. She loved the way his hard planes melded with her softness. Loved the way they felt together, fit together. She linked her wrists around his neck, holding him to her.

His head dipped, accepting her invitation, and he took her mouth with his.

CHAPTER 12

Pen Sutton was like the finest port, mysterious and decadent and utterly intoxicating. Surrendering to the temptation to see her one last time had been a mistake. A thoughtless weakness. But he could not regret it now, with her lips warm and soft and sweet beneath his. Nor could he regret it as he found the pins keeping the glory of her rich auburn hair from him and plucked them away.

Her curls spilled heavy and silken around her shoulders, framing her face, unleashing the soft scent of flowers and seductive woman and *her*. All the hunger and yearning he had so ruthlessly quelled by every means possible rose to the surface, demanding to be answered.

He gave in.

Gave in to the magic that was purely Pen. There was something wondrous about this woman. She was bold and brazen and beautiful, lush in every way a woman ought to be, her body seemingly made for his. But there was also her sharp mind. Her quick wit. He admired her intelligence every bit as much as the rest of her.

He broke the kiss, his breathing harsh, his heart pounding, body aflame, head roaring with desire. The gentleman within him demanded he issue a warning before this progressed too far beyond his control.

"I should go," he said, though those three words cut him like a blade as he issued them.

Her lips were dark and swollen from his kisses, and he knew the driving urge to see her naked beneath him, to watch her hazel eyes as he sank his cock deep inside her.

Those eyes were glazed with passion, fixed on his now. "Stay."

His cock went painfully hard. "If I do, I cannot promise I will be able to put an end to this."

"If you do, I cannot promise I'll want you to put an end to it," she countered, her boldness making him go more rigid still.

He had to have this woman.

On a growl, he kissed her again. Their lips slammed together with a mutual lack of finesse that only served to heighten his need. Her hands were on him, roving over his body with a familiarity that belonged to a lover. Pen Sutton was a woman who knew what she wanted and was not afraid to take it.

And what she wanted now was him. She told him without words, hungrily returning his kisses with an ardor that undid him. Told him as her hands slid inside his coat and urged it off his shoulders. As her clever fingers slipped each button from its mooring on his waistcoat.

The knot of his cravat was next, and when it was gone, she set her lips where it had been, kissing his exposed neck, nipping him with her teeth.

God, yes. He should have known that being with her would be wild. He wanted her mark on him. For her to scratch and bite and suck. His little hellion could have her way with him all she liked.

Together, they worked his shirt over his head, and then they moved to her gown. It was a simple affair, easily removed along with the rest of her garments until she was clad in nothing but a simple chemise, her full breasts straining against the soft fabric. He took a moment to behold her, hair spilling down her back, her arms shapely and creamy, the slimness of her ankles, the perfection, even, of her toes.

"You are beautiful," he rasped.

More beautiful than she had been draped over the French sofa that night. He took her face in his hands and kissed her deeply. Together, they made their way to her bed at the opposite end of the room, mouths fused. When the edge of the mattress abutted his thigh, he paused to whisk away her chemise as well, leaving her completely bare to his roaming, appreciative gaze.

He wanted to be inside her now, to sink his cock into her wet, tight heat. But he had to pace himself, to savor her. He could not devour her all at once. Guiding her hips until her back was to the bed, he urged her to seat herself.

"I want to see you," he said thickly. "To taste you."

He dropped to his knees, longing making his hands tremble as he caressed her waist and then lower, guiding her legs apart. Auburn curls parted as she opened for him. Her cunny was glistening, pink perfection.

His head dipped, fingers sliding through her slickness to allow his tongue to find her plump clitoris. He strummed over it lightly at first, enjoying the way she tasted, musky and womanly with the same hint of flowers that perfumed the rest of her skin. She made a throaty sound of wonder and he licked down her slit to her entrance before thrusting his tongue inside.

He was rewarded by her moaning his name. "Oh, Garrick."

Not Lord Lordly. Not milord. Just Garrick. *Good.* He wanted to simply be a man this evening. To be *her* man.

He returned his attentions to her pearl, latching on to it and sucking as he had done her nipples before. Her reaction was every bit as exquisite. Her hips rocked, undulating against him, as she cried out, her thighs clamping on his head as if to hold him there, just where she wanted him.

He released her, torturing them both by reverting to slow, teasing swipes of his tongue instead. She was deliciously wet and hot as flame, writhing against his mouth with wanton abandon that had him hardening in his trousers. He almost hated that he wore them still, as he was tempted to take himself in hand and stroke. But it was for the best, since he had no wish to spend like a green youth before he had even been inside her.

Instead, he used his fingers to pleasure her, parting her folds to sink into her to the knuckle. Her sweet cunny was drenched, gripping him hard, her body already clenching, then unclenching in the prelude to release. He returned to sucking on her clitoris while the heady sounds of her breathy moans filled the room, mingling with the wetness of his finger as it began to glide in and out in a steady rhythm.

She was tight. So tight, tensed around him. He could not wait to sink into that same inviting wetness with his prick.

Fuck.

He suckled her pearl, then lightly bit as he worked his finger deeper and then added another to join the first, stretching her. Her hips bucked, bringing him to the place she needed, and he thrust high and hard while giving her another long suck. Her release was instant. She tightened on him, nearly coming off the bed as her orgasm rocked through her. He stayed where he was, loving the pulse of her around his fingers, riding out the waves of her pleasure with his lips and teeth and tongue as her dew dripped down his chin.

He was drunk on pleasure.

Drunk on Pen.

But it was still not enough.

He tore his lips from her quim and rose, wiping her juices from his mouth with the back of his hand, feeling like a barbarian as lust and the need to possess her roared through him with libidinous fire. How beautiful she looked, naked and sated, her cheeks flushed, hair wild around her. He wished he could freeze this moment, preserve it in a painting that he might never forget the exact shade of her eyes, the fullness of her lips. That he would never forget the charmed evening she had been his.

Because she never would be again, after this.

He pushed the unwanted reminder aside as she reached for him, her fingers flying over the fall of his trousers, freeing him to her eager touch. And then, although it had never been his intention, she leaned forward, bent her head, and took him into her mouth. Slid from the bed to her knees before him as he clutched at the mattress and willed himself not to explode.

Her lips were soft and silken, exploring him hesitantly. As he looked down to watch the magnificent sight of Pen with her mouth on his cock, she swirled her tongue over the tip, catching a bead of mettle already leaking from his slit. He gripped the bed against a sudden, crushing wave of desire.

If she kept that up, he was not going to last.

"Enough." Gently, he disengaged himself from her, drawing her to her feet.

Her questioning gaze met his, searching. "Have I done it wrong?"

The breath left him in a rush, half laugh, half groan. "Christ no, darling. You have done it quite right. Too right. I do not dare trust myself." He kissed the bridge of her nose to distract himself from the potency of his need.

Her response was to help him off with his trousers. They spilled onto the bed together, wrapped in each other's arms, limbs entangled. Garrick settled them so that Pen was on her back, his body between her thighs, his weight resting on his forearms. He had not come to her tonight to make her his. But now that he was here, body poised to take hers, he could not fathom any other outcome.

He could still taste her on his lips as he bowed his head and took one of her nipples into his mouth. Her hands were on his shoulders, threading through his hair, nails raking down his skin. How right she felt, tucked against him, warm and soft and willing. How very much like his.

For tonight only, he warned himself. Any more than this would be unwise. He had responsibilities awaiting him, a betrothal that could not continue to be indefinitely delayed. But he would fret over that later, when he was capable of coherent thought. Now, all he wanted was the woman in his arms, with her gold-flecked hazel gaze searing into his, lips begging to be kissed.

He took the peak of her other breast into his mouth, loving the sounds she made, the responsive way her body bucked and writhed against his. Garrick's cock was stiff and high against her inner thigh, the warm, silken skin there a brutal tease of what was to come.

He longed to thrust into her, to fill and fuck her, take her hard and fast. But it occurred to him that he did not know just how experienced she was. The women he had known in the past had been far from innocent. He had preferred it that way, for experience rendered the mutual slaking of passion that much more efficient. He had never had cause to wonder.

But although he had once suspected Pen of being a conniving jade, plying her wiles to secure a title and a fortune, he knew he had been wrong about her in more ways than one. He kissed the curve of her breast, charmed by a mole he had failed to notice in the shadows previously. It was shaped like a heart. He flicked his tongue over it, tasting her salt and sweetness.

What a wonder she was.

How had he lived his life thus far without her? How would he live it after?

More unwanted thoughts, chased as he dragged his lips over her collarbone, then up the smooth skin of her throat to her ear. Her fingers glided up and down his back, trailing fire in their wake. He wanted to say something poignant, to praise her, to give voice to the sensations burning through him.

But words were lost.

All he could do was find his way to her lips and claim them with his own. His efforts to prolong the moment crumbled when she reached between them to stroke him. He jerked into her touch, losing more of himself by the moment. Soon, there would be nothing left. He was simply hers.

He leveraged himself onto his left forearm and wrapped his fingers around hers with his free hand, tightening her hold and encouraging her to stroke. *God, yes.* Her hand on him was the devil's work. But sinning had never felt so right, so good, so perfect.

They kissed again, breaths mingling, bodies moving sinuously as one as she brought him dangerously close to the edge of release. On a moan, he tenderly removed her hand, reaching down to toy with her clitoris. Her legs opened wider, and she pumped into his touch, seeking more. He obliged, swirling over the bud until she was coming apart, writhing and reaching her second release.

Only then did he slick her dew over her entrance and his cock both.

Gripping himself, nearly mindless with the need to possess her, he pressed his cock to her soaked cunny. He almost spent then and there, so fierce was the rush of sensation. But this was not enough. He needed more. Had to be inside her.

He thrust, and then he was surrounded by her tight, pulsing heat.

Heaven on earth.

That was what this was, what she was. He had to hold himself still for a moment, to control the roaring need to take her and allow her body to adjust to his. He kissed her throat, the place that drove him to distraction on her—that quivering little hollow at the base where her pulse was racing furiously. He rubbed her pearl with his thumb until she tightened on him, pulling him deeper, her hips tipping upward in a seeking motion. The needy sound in her throat was all he had to hear.

He thrust again, stretching her, filling her. She was all tight, wet heat, constricting on him. He understood without a doubt that he would never know another moment as exquisite as this one, nor another woman. She was meant for him. Made for him. As impossible and wrong as it was, the truth was evident in the way their bodies joined, becoming one. Another thrust, and he was completely inside her, seated deep.

He raised his head and kissed her slowly, lingeringly, and they began to move together, finding their rhythm. His restraint only lasted for a handful of pumps. The combination of her full breasts straining against his chest, her tongue in his mouth, and her cunny clenching on his cock already had him on the brink of orgasm.

He should withdraw. He was going to withdraw. He had every intention of being honorable, of making certain he would not leave Pen with ramifications of this wild night of passion.

But then, her cunny contracted around him, and the sensation was so exquisite, his mind went empty. He forgot everything. His name, his intentions to do right by her, the need to hold tight to the reins of his control. The warmth of her wrapped around his cock, the pulsing of her body, the wetness of her own release, proved far too much.

He came. Emptied himself into her as waves of bliss pounded up his spine and exploded in his skull. The jet of his seed into her body felt right. It was the first time he had ever spent inside a woman, but he did not fool himself that it was the novelty of the sensation that triggered the intensity of his reaction.

Rather, it was the woman beneath him.

Pen.

Garrick held her tight, face pressed to her throat, breathing in her delectable scent, and thrust into her again and again, even when there was nothing left and she had wrung every last drop of mettle from him. Still, he found himself reluctant to withdraw. She felt too good, too perfect.

Gradually, as the lust fled, replaced by the knowledge of what he had done, he realized his error. He had spent inside Pen. Ever since his first, he had been circumspect. Careful to use a sheath and to withdraw for good measure.

Yet he had lost control with her.

Of course he had. Had he believed he would have been able to cling to his restraint in this more than any other matter where she was concerned? What a fool he was. A fool who never should have given in to temptation and come looking for her tonight. A fool who should have made good on his promise to his mother that he would soon be selecting a bride.

Lady Hester.

Her name, like the thought of her, made him go cold. Killed any lingering vestiges of ardor. Ration and reality intruded, sucking the sated languor from him and replacing it with unwanted tension.

Recriminations descended even as Pen held him in the circle of her arms, her heart beating furiously against his chest.

He had no right to do what he had done.

He most definitely should not have kissed her, and he absolutely never should have bedded her. What must she think of him? Hell, he disgusted himself.

He had lost himself with a woman before, and he had vowed he would never do so again. His path in life had been chosen long ago, before Pen had ever entered it.

Duty. That was his path.

Why did that lone word feel so suddenly harsh and cold?

"This was a mistake," he blurted, disengaging from Pen. "Please forgive me."

~

This was a mistake.

Pen rolled away from Viscount Lindsey and rose from the bed, frantic to find her discarded chemise as his words echoed in her mind. She had been reveling in the aftermath of their passion. There had been something perfect about the fit of his cock inside her body, his seed filling her, his chest pressed to hers, his kiss, the wonderful weight of his body pressing hers to the bed. But now, all those feelings had been banished.

How quelling, that sentence.

"Yes, it was a mistake," she agreed coolly, willing away the tears that threatened to fall. She would not allow Lord Lordly to see her weakness for him, to spy her at her most vulnerable. Likely, it would only serve to heighten his already egregious arrogance. "A terrible one."

She found the chemise and threw it over her head, needing to shield herself from him in every way. Allowing him to see her naked for another moment more felt akin to a new sort of betrayal.

"Pen." His voice was concerned, his hand on her lower back intimate.

It was the touch of someone who cared, when he plainly did not. She spun about to face him. "Kindly dress yourself, milord. You'll find the door where you left it when you first trespassed within. Don't let it hit you in the arse on your way out."

"You are angry with me," he said, bending to snap his trousers over his calves and hips.

Lord, where was a vase when one needed to hurl it at a scurrilous viscount's head?

She was so furious, she could not hide the trembling in her voice or her hands as she donned her discarded petticoat and attempted to fasten it.

"His lordship deserves a prize for his astute powers of observation," she snapped, unable to keep the bitterness from her tone or her heart. Only he would dare to pleasure her to the edge of reason, only to claim it had all been a mistake and revert to drawing room etiquette. "How politely you speak, as if we are perfect strangers meeting at an assembly room rather than a man and woman who were just fucking."

He flinched at her use of the vulgar word, but the sight of his disapproval provided no delight. She had come of age in the halls and gaming rooms of this gaming hell and in the darkened alleys of the rookeries. She knew words—and likely deeds as well—that would make his lordly toes curl in his Hessians.

"What happened between us now was not..." He paused, then shook his head. "It was more than that."

Yes, she most certainly had believed it had been.

Until he had opened his beautiful mouth and dashed her heart to bits for the second time.

She pinned a cold smile to her lips. "Let us not pretend, my lord. We have been dancing about this desire burning between us ever since you appeared here at The Sinner's Palace, calling me everything but a lady. We wanted each other, and now we have had each other. Our curiosity has been sated. I thank you for the evening's diversion, but you really ought to go now."

He pulled his shirt over his head, robbing her of the view of his well-muscled chest and flat abdomen. It was just as well. Her stupid body could not seem to tell that he was crushing her heart into dust. But what had she expected would come of allowing him into her bed? A declaration of love?

Had she believed, even for a moment, that the august Viscount Lindsey would deem her worthy of himself when he had not even believed her good enough for his youngest brother? Hardly.

He reached for her, but she danced away, leaving him to retrieve his wrinkled cravat from the floor with an air of reluctance. "Curse it, Pen, let me explain."

"I think you have done quite enough talking," she snapped, her voice going shrill in her attempts at maintaining her composure, which grew more difficult by the second.

She was filled with self-loathing. How had she allowed herself to be so weak? He was everything her brothers had warned her against, every reason why they told her the quality was never to be trusted. Why she was meant to stay far, far away from all lords. And yet she had fallen neatly into his trap. Yet another conquest for him. An East End fortune hunter he instantly regretted making love to the moment he had drained his ballocks.

"Perhaps you have no wish to hear it, but I am going to tell you anyway," he countered, commanding her gaze.

He had donned his gleaming boots and was only lacking his coat, which still lay on her floor. The wickedest part of her briefly imagined tossing it into the grate and watching it catch flame from the fireplace's flickering embers. It would serve him right to leave without all his rum rigging.

"I'm not accustomed to this much prattle from men after we make the beast with two backs," she lied, knowing it was childish and yet wanting to hurt him just the same. Needing to lash him with her words as he had done to her. "I am growing weary of the noise."

His nostrils flared at her insult. "Do not think to fool me. You were a virgin when I took you."

"Rather conceited of you to think yourself the first," she taunted. "You didn't really believe I'd give myself so easily if I hadn't already done it many times before, did you?"

In truth, she and Daniel had kissed and otherwise touched. But he had never claimed her body as Garrick had. No other man had done, for she had never wanted it with them. When she had loved Daniel, she had been far too young, and he had chosen Gertrude Cholmley over her when she had refused him further liberties.

But she would sooner throw herself from the window to the putrid streets below than admit as much to the man who had just made love to her and then called it a mistake.

"It matters not if you did," Garrick told her, moving toward Pen once again. "You could have taken a hundred lovers before me, and what I did still would have been wrong."

"Wrong," she repeated, the word joining all the others

before as yet another barb to pierce her heart. "So you have said. A mistake. Wrong. I understand, my lord. You regret lying with someone such as myself, whom you perceive as so far beneath you that the notion your brother would have wished to make me his wife meant I was some sort of fortune-seeking whore."

He flinched as if she had slapped him. "You mistake me, Pen. What happened between us is wrong because I am meant to be marrying someone else."

I am meant to be marrying someone else.

Marrying someone else.

Someone else.

Another woman. Someone who was not her. But then, once again, why should she be surprised? He was the heir to the Duke of Dryden. Of course he would have found the loveliest diamond of the first water to become his future duchess. Likely the daughter of a duke herself.

His words echoed in Pen's mind, taunting her, this round far more jagged, sharp, and likely to make her bleed than the first. She swallowed against a rush of bile. How lovely to know he considered bedding her a mistake because he was going to be taking another woman as his wife. He may as well have cut her beating heart from her breast and tossed it into the fire.

"I never should have touched you for that reason," he added. "It was not just dishonorable of me, but it went against every tenet I hold dear as a gentleman."

"Ah, your honor," she repeated, feeling as brittle as her voice sounded. "And your gentlemanly tenets. Those should not be betrayed, should they?"

And neither, she longed to say, *should I.*

But she held her tongue and kept her head high, refusing to show him how devastated she was on the inside.

"Pen," he tried, reaching for her again.

Half an hour ago, she would have taken that hand, threaded her fingers through his, and followed him anywhere. But half an hour ago, she had believed the best of him, and he had swiftly proven her wrong.

So very wrong.

She shook her head, refusing him. "Go now, Lord Lindsey. Go before you make this worse."

Her heart had splintered into so many shards that she could not even summon the desire to mock him. First, he had been Lord Lordly to her, then Garrick, and now? Now, he was merely Lord Lindsey. Just as he always should have been.

He studied her, those bright-blue aristocrat's eyes plumbing the depths of hers. She stood still for the examination, willing her countenance to remain lifeless. To refuse to show him even a hint of the hurt and pain he had dealt her. Nothing of the love she felt for him, burning like a hot coal still. He did not deserve it.

He did not deserve *her*.

But while he had not been the first man who was unworthy of her heart, he would most definitely be the last. And whatever it was he saw in her eyes apparently persuaded him that the time for conversation between them was done.

He gave a jerky nod. "If that is what you wish."

She inclined her head, hoping she looked regal instead of downtrodden. Hoping he would think of her every moment he spent in the company of his future wife and that he forever regretted his decision.

"It is what I wish," she told him. "Farewell, my lord."

He bowed, and then, he left her room, taking her heart with him.

CHAPTER 13

Pen bid a good morrow to the painters plying their trade in the main entrance of The Sinner's Palace II, the club she and her siblings were opening in the West End. Her voice did not even crack, which pleased her mightily. If any of the workers suspected she had spent the entire evening in tears, or that her heart had been ground beneath the Hessians of a diabolically handsome viscount the night before, they were too wise to comment upon it.

She breezed by them, feigning calm when inside, she was a storm-tossed sea. She had not slept. When she had finally given in to her restlessness at dawn and splashed water on her face to cool her swollen eyes and heated cheeks, she had determined that continuing on the ledgers would not do for distraction today. Fortunately, she had more work to keep her mind and hands busy here at the new club.

As the eldest sister who was not occupied with a husband, the task of decorating had fallen to Pen's discretion. She had been initially resentful over the additional responsibilities. Her sister Caroline was happily married to Gavin Winter, the famed prizefighter, and was only called upon for her healing talents. Lily was the youngest and thoroughly cossetted. Her brother Jasper's wife was occupied with seeing to her nieces' welfare, and none of her other brothers were yet wed, though she suspected her brother Rafe's diminished presence at The Sinner's Palace II heralded a coming change.

It all left Pen to see about such details as linens, paints, and wall hangings at the new club. And she was throwing herself into the duty awaiting her with enthusiasm and a desperate need to forget all about Lord Lindsey.

And forget him, she would.

If it was the last thing she did.

Casting an eye about to make certain the paint colors looked well enough in the main hall, she was soon interrupted.

"Miss Sutton?"

Pen turned to find one of the guards from The Sinner's Palace who was on duty directing the tradesmen this morning approaching her.

"Bennet," she greeted, pleased for further distraction, even if she did not feel at all like smiling when she forced her mouth into some semblance of the gesture. "I have missed seeing you at The Sinner's Palace these last few days."

He grunted. "I was there yesterday, miss."

Oh dear.

"Forgive me," she said, and then could have winced for the manner in which she seemed to unintentionally be parroting the viscount's words the night before. "I do recall seeing you there, now that you mention it."

In truth, she did not, but she felt it imperative to treat everyone in her family's employ at The Sinner's Palace as if they were an extension of the Suttons. With respect and appreciation and a good dose of cheer.

To his credit, Bennet nodded. Like many of the men working for The Sinner's Palace, he had been plucked from the streets and a life of crime. "The linen draper's come early, Miss Sutton."

The linen draper. More distraction. Wonderful.

"Bring him to me, Bennet."

With a nod, the man disappeared, leaving Pen to continue on with her examination of the progress at the new club. She moved through halls and rooms in various state of repair and change, until she reached the largest chamber, which would become the main gaming room of their establishment. It was the most complete chamber in the building, smelling of fresh paint, with gaming tables already adorning the new carpets.

She should have been pleased by the sight. Pleased at the prospect of future success for the Sutton family within these walls. And yet, as she glanced around her surroundings, all she felt was…numb.

Before she could wallow in her thoughts for too long, Bennet reappeared, the linen draper in tow.

Mr. Waters was red-cheeked, rotund, and possessed the smug air of masculine superiority she despised. He looked over her shoulder, then about the room after Bennet announced him, as if he were searching for someone else.

"And where is Mr. Sutton this morning?" he asked.

His query nettled her. She was more than accustomed to being undervalued because of her sex.

She forced a smile. "I am Miss Sutton, Mr. Sutton's sister, and one of the owners of this establishment."

Mr. Waters frowned. "I was given to understand I would be meeting with your brother, madam."

She had requested the meeting herself the previous week, and long before she had known how desperately she would need to distract herself today, in an effort to show him where the gaming tables would be placed. But she had no doubt he had simply misread the missive.

"You are meeting with me," she gritted. "Thank you,

Bennet. I will call for you if you are needed." She waited for the guard to leave before turning her attention back to Mr. Waters. "If you please, have you brought any samples with you?"

The case he carried on his back suggested he had.

With a look of distaste, he unfastened it, extracting a plain table linen which seemed of reasonable quality, extending it to her for inspection.

It hardly appeared worthy of the dear price he was charging. And worst of all, it was plain. She turned the linen over in her hands to be certain before glancing back up at the merchant. "I requested embroidery on each table cloth, but there is none on this one."

"I am afraid I cannot provide the embroidery within the time your brother has specified, Miss Sutton," Mr. Waters said dispassionately, stoking her ire.

Was that not just like a man to promise far more than he could provide? To charm and deceive without a hint of compunction? She looked into the merchant's eyes and knew he had never intended to provide the embroidery she had asked for—the silhouette of a palace in blue stitch—at all. And nor did he give a damn that he would not be providing it.

Perhaps it was the scorched ash in her heart. Or perhaps it was a life spent lived in the shadows of her brothers, always being overlooked and ignored by men such as Mr. Waters because she was a woman. Or mayhap it was both.

Whatever the reason, Pen was furious.

So outraged, her hand shook as she presented Mr. Waters with his inferior cloth. "This is wholly unacceptable, sir. We are paying for embroidery."

"Embroidery was never promised," he said.

"It was promised," she countered.

"Not by myself," he blustered.

She clenched her jaw. "The embroidery aside, how many cloths do you have at the ready?"

"Twenty, as promised," he said, further proving his incompetence.

"We require two-and-thirty, sir, as you well know."

She suppressed the urge to scream to the rafters. In the next moment, her older brother Rafe had arrived, his blond curls framing his face and giving him an angelic air that was decidedly the opposite of the devoted rogue he was.

"Pen?" he asked, seemingly surprised to find her within, at odds with the linen draper.

"Rafe, come here if you please," she invited, relieved for some aid, "and explain to Mr. Waters why we cannot have inferior table cloths at our establishment. I have brought him here to show him the precise locations of the tables, and he now insists he cannot have the embroidery we require within the next month."

"Mr. Sutton," said Mr. Waters, suddenly obsequious. "Perhaps you can provide the voice of reason, sir. Miss Sutton's demands are, regretfully, nigh impossible to achieve."

Rake looked from Pen to Mr. Waters. "What's the problem?"

"I want all the table cloths to be embroidered with a palace," she explained.

"A palace embroidered on each cloth?" Rafe repeated, passing his hand along his jaw as if contemplating how dear a price such a table linen would fetch.

"Only think how it will set us apart from our competitors," Pen pointed out, knowing her brother far too well.

"I have all the linens you originally purchased at the ready," Mr. Waters declared. "But as for the embroidery, I must ask for an increase of price and far more time. I won't be capable of producing the number requested with the embroidery before you open your establishment, and Miss Sutton refuses to accept this."

An increase in price? Why, the man put highwaymen and pickpockets to shame. His original price had contained the embroidery! She was sure she had a note back at The Sinner's Palace to prove it.

"I won't accept it because your excuse simply isn't good enough, Mr. Waters," she told the man firmly. "If you refuse to give us what we need, then we will take our business to someone who will."

"You ought to consider yourself fortunate to have Waters and Sons linen gracing your tables," the draper said coldly, directing his words to Rafe, quite as if Pen were not even present in the room.

Oh, to punch the man in his bulbous nose. He would deserve it. And worse. And whilst she was about the task, why not plant Lord Lindsey a facer as well? No man in all London was owed one more!

"We will accept the linens you've already agreed to provide, Mr. Waters," her brother said smoothly.

How *dare* he?

"We most certainly will not!" Pen snapped, outraged. "Mr. Waters, you can take your pompous airs and your plain tablecloths and stuff them up your—"

"That is enough, Penelope!" Rafe barked, interrupting. "Please excuse my sister, sir. Our order remains the same."

Flashing his scoundrel's grin, Rafe hastened to escort Mr. Waters from the room as Pen watched on, feeling ineffectual. Ignored. Utterly worthless in every way.

She had come here to The Sinner's Palace II to find distraction and validation, and instead, she had found more of the same. More humiliation. More of a man who believed himself her superior looking down his nose at her.

She sniffled, and whether it was the lack of sleep, her

broken heart, her frustration with Mr. Waters, or all three, she could not say. But once the tears she had been tamping down ever since she had dried the last bout emerged, she could not stay them. They were running down her cheeks by the time her brother returned.

"What is amiss, Pen?" he asked, arriving at her side.

Her inner turmoil was not entirely her brother's fault, but he was going to pay for the most recent contribution to it, that was certain.

"How dare you undermine me?" she asked, swiping at her cheeks. "He had the number of tablecloths wrong, and I fail to understand why he cannot provide the embroidery. He asked me where *Mr. Sutton* was when he arrived."

A fresh wave of tears punctuated her words, and she did nothing to hide them.

Rafe extracted a handkerchief, offering it to her. "You need to calm yourself, Pen. The tables will be filled regardless of whether or not there is a bit of thread stitched in a palace on them."

She snatched the scrap of linen from him and dabbed at her cheeks. "Men are nothing but a great bloody lot of arrogant loggerheads!"

"Is this about Lord Aidan Weir, Pen?" he asked.

Lord Aidan? Ha! If only…

"Of course not." She sniffled. "It's his brother the haughty arse who…" She caught herself and stayed the rampant flow of words.

No need to tell her protective older brother what had happened. Or anyone else. Ever.

Too late.

Rafe's brows rose. "His brother? Which one?"

She shook her head. "It hardly matters now. I'll not be seeing Lord Lindsey again."

Her brother scowled. "That is for the best, sister."

"Of course it is," she agreed, forcing a smile to her lips, because it *was* for the best, regardless of how much her heart was aching right now. "But never mind his high and mighty lordship. We have a gaming hell to open."

"Indeed we do, and we'd both do well to keep our minds on The Sinner's Palace II where they belong," Rafe said, patting her on the back.

Yes, she would be better served to only think about their new establishment and not at all about the man who had made love to her the night before, only to call it a mistake and tell her he intended to marry someone else.

She inhaled slowly, willing all the pain and hurt away. "Lead the way, brother."

~

In his mother's favorite sitting room at Dryden House, Garrick took a sip of perfectly prepared tea and wondered how he ought to inform his mother and father that he was about to create the scandal of the century. Father's color was good today; he was not pale as he had been on Garrick's previous visit, when Aidan had announced his plans to marry Miss Penelope Sutton. Garrick's own announcement, not long after, was bound to cause some upset.

He had to proceed with caution.

"The news from Dr. Wilton is good?" he asked Father casually.

It was the polite way of inquiring whether or not he might render his sire apoplectic when he revealed the purpose of his call.

"It is cautious, but promising," his father said.

"His Grace has not had to use the Bath chair for several days now," Mother added, sending a small smile in her husband's direction as she idly stroked an orange cat which had settled in her lap.

"That is excellent to hear," Garrick said, wishing he were partaking of something stronger than tea, although he scarcely ever imbibed.

Part of him felt lighter than he ever had, filled with the brightness of a thousand suns. But part of him felt heavy, his gut tangled in knots. Knots for the way he had left Pen the night before. Knots for her fury with him. Knots for the unburdening he needed to do today. He had already made one call, to Lady Hester, which had been easier than he had supposed.

As it turned out, Lady Hester had set her cap at the Earl of Carlington, and she was hoping for an understanding to be reached any day. She and Garrick had parted as friends. He was not certain he would be so blessed by a similarly pleasant outcome on this occasion.

Mother had set her heart upon Lady Hester as his bride.

But he was not in love with Lady Hester. And leaving her earlier had not made his heart feel as if it were shattering into irreparable shards in his chest as it had when he had left Pen the night before.

"My lord?" Mother was prompting him, cutting through his thoughts.

A lack of sleep and the weight of what he must do had rendered his mind sluggish. He blinked, attempting to chase away his distraction. "Yes, Mother?"

"You were wool-gathering," she observed tartly, giving the feline a scratch between the ears. "I asked if you had heard Aidan's news."

"Aidan's news?" He frowned, wondering what manner of madcap nonsense his brother had managed to entangle himself in now, and so soon after he had just been rescued from the devious Mrs. Knightly.

"We are to wish him happy," Father said in a tone of resignation. "He has decided he will wed the unsuitable Miss Sutton after all."

The lack of fury in his father's tone and the absence of outraged color flooding to his cheeks would have pleased Garrick, for it hardly seemed as if his father would suffer another of his fits on account of Aidan's antics. However, the words he heard were wrong. It took a moment for them to permeate Garrick's sleep-deprived brain.

He returned his teacup to its saucer with more force than necessary and straightened in his chair. "Forgive me, but I fear I misheard you, Father."

"You did not mishear," Mother said, voice dripping with distaste. "Your brother wishes to marry Miss Mutton."

"Sutton," he corrected absently.

"Mutton, Sutton, Button." His mother made a dismissive gesture. "The name hardly signifies. The ensuing scandal, however, does. You may as well prepare yourself, my lord. And warn Lady Hester, as well. We have tried to dissuade him, but he seems unwilling to stray from his course for a second time. I had so hoped he was finally willing to see reason when he told us the betrothal had been broken."

Damn it, Aidan still wanted to marry Pen despite their conversation at Rivendale's. He had hoped his brother would reconsider.

A possessive surge went through him then. Pen was *his,* damn it.

"Impossible," he bit out. "It will never happen."

"At least one of our sons sees reason," Mother quipped.

"Aidan cannot marry Miss Sutton," he elaborated, "because I am."

At least, he hoped he was. He had yet to ask her. After suffering through a sleepless night, he had made an early-morning visit to Winter's Boxing Academy. Garrick had returned home with aching knuckles and the certain knowledge that Pen Sutton owned his heart, and that he could not bear to live without her.

"*You* are?" Mother's voice was high and shrill, steeped in disbelief.

"Yes." And how freeing that one word, that revelation, was.

He had spent the years since Veronica's betrayal attempting to be the son his parents wanted, the lord society expected him to be. A stickler for propriety. The perfect gentleman. He had done everything right. But on the inside… On the inside, he had been hollow. He had been joyless and frigid.

Pen had filled him with warmth and happiness. She had taught him that loving again was worth the risk, any risk. Society and its expectations could go to the devil for all he cared. He was not going to marry Lady Hester Torshell. He was going to marry the woman he loved.

Yes, *loved*.

He loved Pen Sutton.

Had loved her, quite possibly, from the moment she had stormed into her office at The Sinner's Palace and demanded to know who he was.

"I do not understand," his mother was saying, distraught. "What hold does this horrid creature have over the both of you?"

"Miss Sutton is neither horrid nor a creature," he corrected her coolly. "She is an intelligent woman who is deserving of your respect, not your disdain."

His mother was sputtering, disturbing the cat on her lap. "But she is common. Worse than common. How could you wish to bind yourself to an East End vagabond?"

"Need I remind you of your origins?" his father asked sternly. "You were a merchant's daughter when we married."

His mother gasped as if she had been struck.

Garrick glanced from his father to his mother, shocked himself. He had always believed his mother had been the daughter of a country baron. At least, that was the tale she told. He had never known his grandparents, both having died before he was born.

"You are the daughter of a Cit?" he asked her now.

"Do not speak to me of it." She pressed a hand to her brow. "I am feeling faint. Fetch me my hartshorn."

What an interesting development this was. His mother had been keeping a secret, it would seem. A very large, potentially useful one.

Garrick found himself grinning. "Given your experience, Mother, I have no doubt you will prove helpful in aiding my wife to find her footing in polite society."

She issued a heavy sigh. "I expected better of you, my lord. What of Lady Hester?"

"Lady Hester wishes to marry Carlington," he said, still smiling. "Which is fortunate indeed, for I have every intention of wedding Miss Sutton if she will have me."

If his mother had weathered the storm of her own murky past to become one of the leading arbiters of Society, why could not Pen also manage the same? It was true that her family was…unique. But Garrick did not give a damn. He was going to live life as he pleased, unfettered by society's dictates. He was going to love, and damn the consequences.

"There is one problem," Father said. "You and Aidan cannot both marry the same woman."

Yes, there was that. He needed to find Pen and his brother with all haste to sort this muddle out. But first, he needed to know something. He was going to marry Pen regardless of the answer to his next question as long as she would forgive him for the manner in which he had bungled matters the night before. But knowing how much of a challenge they faced from his parents would be a boon.

He searched his father's countenance. "Do I have your blessing?"

"All I want is to see my sons happy," Father said quietly, his customary sternness fading.

Garrick swallowed against a rush of emotion and nodded. "Thank you, Father."

He was on his feet and striding for the door in the next moment, his mother's voice trailing after him.

"Your sons shall be the death of me, I fear, Your Grace."

"They are your sons also," Father was reminding.

"Only when they please me," she grumbled.

CHAPTER 14

"While I was tied to that bed, I had a great deal of time to think about everything," Aidan was saying, his expression earnest. "Time to think about you and how much your friendship means to me and how bloody selfish I have been. It was unfair of me to use you to anger my family, and I admit it. It was also wrong of me to want to marry you when I had no intention of remaining faithful. You deserve so much better than that, so much better than me."

Pen had returned from The Sinner's Palace II to find her friend awaiting her in the parlor, looking sheepish and requesting a word.

But this was decidedly *not* what she had anticipated. An invitation to another bare-knuckle match, or a covert expedition to The Garden of Flora, mayhap. An apology that was alarmingly close to a declaration, however? No.

She had a sick feeling she knew where this conversation was heading, and she had to stop it before it went too far. "I am certain you had time aplenty to consider everything that had happened, but I am not upset with you, Aidan. I never planned to marry you, and you know that."

"So you told me, but I was hoping you would—*will*—change your mind." He reached for her hand.

This was new, a gesture of affection between them. For the entirety of their friendship, Aidan had been a reckless, silly rakehell with not a modicum of seriousness in him. His attentions had never been amorous in nature. Indeed, until he had formulated his ludicrous notion they get betrothed to anger his family, Pen had been hard-pressed to believe he even saw her as a female. On most occasions when they were together, she dressed as a cove to hide her true identity.

She tried to tug her hand from his, but he clung steadfastly.

"Whatever do you mean, Aidan?" she asked. "What is there to change my mind about?"

"About me." He gave her fingers a squeeze. "About us."

Us?

Good heavens.

"I care about you as my friend," she reassured him, "just as I always have. However, there is no us, Aidan. There never has been, nor shall there ever be."

"How can you be so certain? We have never tried to make there be an us." He shook his head. "I should have courted you properly. I would like to do so now, if you would permit it."

Aidan wanted to court her.

Meanwhile, his brother, the man she loved, wanted nothing to do with her. He had made love to her, announced it had been a mistake, and then professed his intention to marry someone else. A suitable bride, no doubt. A perfectly groomed, wealthy lady who knew how to curtsy and dance and play the pianoforte. How Pen hated that lady, whomever she was.

How she longed to be her.

But Aidan was watching her now, awaiting her response.

"You must know I care for you. Heavens, if I didn't, I would have happily given you a basting after all the troubles you caused me. But I am in love with someone else."

"You are?" He almost sounded slightly relieved.

He probably was. Knowing Aidan, this was some sort of addle-pated means of making amends for the recent tangle he had made of her life.

"Yes," she said, thinking of Garrick as her heart squeezed painfully. "Unfortunately, I am."

She was in love with the wrong brother, and he would never love her in return.

"Why do you say unfortunately?" Aidan was still holding her hand, but Pen felt nary a spark, no hint of awareness.

Only Garrick could move her, it seemed.

"Because the man I love does not love me," she said, biting her lip to stave off a rush of tears.

She would not weep over a hardhearted, arrogant lord.

She would not.

A tear slipped down her cheek.

She was, blast it all.

"Dash the blighter," Aidan said, releasing her hand to reach into his coat and extract a handkerchief and offer it to her. "He does not deserve you either."

She sniffed, trying to keep the waterworks at bay and failing. "No, he does not."

She should have told him so last night. But then, she never should have been so foolish as to fall in love with Garrick in the first place.

"Are you certain you do not wish to marry me, then?" Aidan waggled his brows at her in comical fashion.

Pen laughed though her tears. For all that he had unwittingly put her on the path that had led to her broken heart,

Aidan was dear to her. He could exasperate and charm simultaneously. It was one of his talents.

"It would not be fair to you," she said. "There is only one man I want to marry, and he is marrying another."

"Who?"

The low, familiar voice shot through the room. Pen's gaze flew to the door of the parlor where Garrick stood, tall, dignified, and heartbreakingly handsome. Every inch the perfect lord. She shot to her feet, scrubbing at her cheeks with the handkerchief in a hasty attempt at drying them and hiding her sadness from him.

"Brother," Aidan greeted, rising.

Garrick nodded, but his gaze was riveted upon Pen. Cold, blue, austere.

Haunting.

She had not been prepared to see him again so soon. Or ever. Her heart thudded fast.

"You said there is only one man you want to marry," Garrick said. "Who is he?"

She crumpled the scrap of linen in her fist and straightened her posture. "Why should you care?"

"Yes indeed, why should you care?" Aidan's gaze flitted between Pen and Garrick, his brow furrowed. "I thought the two of you scarcely were acquainted."

Pen flashed a tight smile. "We are quite *familiar,* your brother and I. Are we not, my lord?"

Just last night, they had been as familiar as a man and woman could be to each other.

Garrick strode forward, entering the parlor, closing the distance between them, his gaze never wavering as he stopped just short of Pen and Aidan. "Yes, we are."

She vowed she would not take a single step in retreat. She would be strong. But oh, how difficult it was to try to remain impervious. Her heart was his, even after last night. It would always, forever, belong to him.

"Christ, Garrick," Aidan said into the silence. "Have you been dallying with Pen?"

Was it that obvious? How humiliating. The urge to flee the chamber and lock herself away was strong, just barely quelled.

Garrick flicked a glance in Aidan's direction. "Leave us, brother."

"I am not certain I should." Aidan turned to Pen. "Tell me what you want, and I'll do it."

She glanced back at Garrick, heart torn. What could he possibly require of her? Why had he returned to The Sinner's Palace?

"Please, Pen," he entreated softly, devoid of his customary arrogance. "A few moments of your time is all I beg."

"Pen?" Aidan prodded.

She inhaled slowly, her breath hitching with a humiliating sob. Part of her wanted to salvage her pride and tell Garrick to go to the devil. But part of her was desperate to know why he had returned.

"You may leave us," Pen relented. "I shan't be in any harm."

Her heart, however, was another matter.

Aidan searched her gaze, then nodded, apparently seeing what he needed to see reflected there. "I'll go. But know this, brother, if you are the one responsible for making Pen weep, you had damn well better make amends for it."

Thank you, Aidan, she thought grimly. If Garrick had not noticed she had been weeping when he arrived before, there was no question of it now.

"I will," Garrick said solemnly.

How? She wanted to ask, but her tattered pride would not allow it. Instead, she held her tongue and watched her friend take his leave before reluctantly looking back to the man she loved.

Which proved a mistake, for he was gazing at her in a new way. The icy lordly mask of indifference was gone, and in its place was something different. Dare she think it tenderness?

"Who?" he asked again.

And he did not have to elaborate, for she knew what he wanted from her. The name of the man she wanted to marry.

The prick of tears began anew in her eyes. "Do you need to hear me say it?"

He moved closer, reaching for her hands, and took them in his. "Yes."

He was wearing gloves, but his warmth seared her, bringing a rush of longing for him back to life. She wanted to pull away. To disengage and run from him. But a splinter of hope remained, burrowed in her heart, telling her to stay.

To tell him the truth.

To take the risk.

"You," she admitted, tears burning her eyes and rendering her words halting. "It is you. Are you happy now?"

He smiled slowly, tugging her against his chest. "I could be happier."

"I am certain you shall be whenever you marry your beautiful aristocratic bride," she said, unable to keep the bitterness from her voice.

"I am not marrying Lady Hester."

Her heart leapt, but she forced it to calm. "That's a rum choice, because her name is quite dreadful."

He chuckled. "Her name matters not. She is in love with the Earl of Carlington, which is a most fortuitous turn of fortune's fickle wheel, because I am also in love with another."

She froze. "Oh?"

Please let her be me.

"Yes." He brought her fingers to his lips for a reverent kiss. "Perhaps you know her."

She swallowed. "I hope I do."

Icy-blue eyes burned into hers. "She is bold and daring and intelligent. She is not afraid to speak her mind or face a villain with a pistol. She has an excellent head for keeping ledgers, she has a mouth I long to kiss every hour of every day, the most glorious auburn hair I have ever beheld, and mysterious hazel eyes flecked with gold. She is known for gadding about London dressed as a gentleman, she is a brave and loyal friend, and from the moment I first met her, she has owned not just my thoughts, but my heart as well."

Oh.

Oh.

She was speechless. Those persistent tears returned, prickling her eyes. But this time, they were tears of happiness. He was speaking of *her*.

"I believe," she managed weakly, "that we may be acquainted."

"You are." He released her hands and cupped her face. "Because she is *you*. I love you, Pen Sutton. I have spent the last few years being the man society expected of me. But I want to spend the rest of my life being *your* man, if you will have me."

"You love me," she repeated, afraid to trust those words. Afraid to believe them.

And yet, needing to so badly, it was a physical ache.

"I love you," he said again. "Will you marry me?"

Yes! It was there, on her tongue, but she suppressed it. She had spent every moment since he had left her the night before in agony, and he needed to answer for it.

"Just last night, you said what happened between us was a mistake," she reminded him.

"Last night, I was an arse, and I must beg your forgiveness." His gaze roamed hers, love shining in those brilliant depths. "What happened between us was a mistake because I should have waited until I was your husband to make love to you. I should have had some honor and restraint, but where you are concerned, it would seem I have none. Nothing can keep me from wanting you to be mine. Not the belief you were betrothed to my brother, not my parents, not the *ton*, not Lady Hester. Nothing and no one can keep me from loving you."

He loved her.

Garrick *loved* her.

But as much as his words filled her with hope and happiness, the vast disparities in their worlds had not disappeared.

"I was born in the East End," she forced herself to say. "I will never be a lady."

"You are a lady in every way that matters," he countered. "I want you and only you."

"Your society will scorn me," she added. "If you feared the scandal Aidan marrying me would have caused, what do you think would happen if *you* were to marry me? You will be a duke one day."

"I will be a duke who is madly in love with his duchess," he said gently.

"Tongues will wag," she continued. "You know it as well as I do. A lord as prominent as yourself cannot wed an East End Sutton without being disparaged."

"Let the tongues wag. Let the gossip mongers spread their scandal broth. All I want to do is love you. Marry me, Pen."

He was intent upon his course, resolute. And she was weary of trying to dissuade him. The events of the previous night, a lack of sleep, and heartache all battered away at the crumbling walls of her defenses.

"I love you too," she conceded at last. "And I would be honored to be your wife."

"I told you I could be happier," he said, grinning. "And you have made me so. You'll not regret it, Pen. I swear. I will do my utmost to be the husband you deserve."

"I believe you, Lord Lordly," she teased, smiling against a rush of joyous tears this time.

"Hoyden." He kissed her crown, no sting in the word. "What am I to do with you?"

She pretended to ponder his question before smiling up at him, love filling her with a new, previously undiscovered sense of wonder. "Kiss me first. And then make me your Lady Lordly."

"With pleasure," he said, before his lips sealed over hers.

EPILOGUE

"I have never been more relieved in my life."

With a sigh of contentment, Pen arranged her skirts beside her new husband in the carriage that was conveying them from Dryden House, where they had married before a small group of family and friends, to Garrick's town house. This time, she would not be secreted within via a dark corridor designed by viscounts past to hide their illicit affairs. Instead, she would be entering through the front door, and not as a guest disguised in trousers, either.

No indeed, she would be introduced as the new Lady Lindsey.

Or as she preferred to think of her title, Lady Lordly.

It never failed to make her smile. But then, so did Lord Lordly himself.

"Nor have I." Garrick lowered his head and took her lips in a possessive kiss that was far too brief for her liking. "I thought the wedding and the damnable breakfast afterward would never end."

Both formalities had indeed seemed endless, particularly

when Pen's siblings and Garrick's family had rendered it impossible for them to spend time alone together during their betrothal. The freedom to be alone with him, to touch him, was a much-appreciated wonder.

"I could not wait to be alone with you," she confessed. "I have missed you, my love."

"Surely not more than I have missed you, darling." He caught her cheek in one gloved hand and caressed her jaw. "The wait to become your husband has been bleeding interminable."

She chuckled. "You have been spending too much time in the company of my brothers. You have taken on their manner of speech."

"I had to spend time with them if I was to be near you," he said wryly, kissing her again, more slowly this time, his lips brushing back and forth over hers with painstaking care.

"You were not near enough," she pointed out, breathless when the kiss was done. "My brothers never took note when I was going about London dressed as a cove, but the moment I was betrothed to a lord, they decided to play chaperone like a set of maiden aunts."

Of her brothers, Hart and Wolf had been the most dedicated to their brotherly duties. Jasper and Rafe were both far too preoccupied with their new wives to care whether or not she was alone with Garrick in the parlor at The Sinner's Palace. Hart and Wolf, however, had proved merciless. She had quite lost count of the number of kisses they had interrupted during her betrothal.

Fortunately, Garrick had secured a special license, which meant they had not been required to wait nearly as long as they otherwise would have to be man and wife.

"You are right. It was never near enough, was it?" His hand snaked around her waist, and in a trice, he had hauled her onto his lap. "Let us make up for lost opportunities, shall we?"

She found herself astride him, the position bringing her aching intimate flesh into contact with his trousers in delightful, wicked fashion. "I thought the trip to your town house would not be long."

He buried his face in her throat and inhaled as if she were a life-granting breath of air. "I've instructed Neave to take three tours of Mayfair. I cannot introduce you to the servants and then haul you over my shoulder to bed you senseless as I would like, so this shall have to suffice in the interim."

She clasped his broad shoulders and undulated against him as the carriage rolled over a particularly facilitating set of bumps. That felt positively divine. But not as divine as he would feel inside her.

"What a wicked man you are, Lord Lordly," she said with mock indignation. "The most proper lord in London certainly has fallen from grace."

"I would not have it any other way." He cupped her breast through the bodice of her gown.

She was not wearing stays, and the warmth of his hand burned through the layers of fabric separating them in tempting fashion. When he rolled her aching nipple between his thumb and forefinger, she gasped in pleasure.

"Nor would I," she admitted.

His bright gaze dipped to her décolletage, his stare as heady as a caress. "During the entirety of the ceremony, I was watching your breasts in this gown, wondering what would happen if I gave the bodice a stern tug."

She was breathless in truth now, her heart pounding, her sex pulsing and wet. "Perhaps you should find out."

He caught her bodice in both hands and pulled it down. Her breasts popped free of the diaphanous fabric, still trapped within her chemise. That undergarment was lowered with hasty motions until her breasts were cupped beneath by both her gown and chemise, held high like offerings for his delectation.

On a growl, he took one of her nipples into his mouth. She rocked over his already rigid cock. The carriage swayed, and she hoped Neave could not hear the sounds they made. But she was also too shameless to care if he could. She had waited far too long to be bedded by her husband, and like him, she was feverish with need.

Sucking on the peak of her other breast, he began lifting the skirt of her gown until it and the petticoats beneath reached her waist. He raised his head from her breast, before catching the forefinger of his glove in his teeth and tugging. First one hand, then the other until his hands were bare.

And then, those knowing fingers were upon her, caressing a path of fire up the insides of her thighs, one reaching to massage a cheek of her bottom while the other dipped between her folds to play.

"My lady is wet," he said, his voice low and soft as velvet.

His proclamation made her wetter still, and so did his fingers as they unerringly discovered her pearl. He swirled over the sensitive bud, sending pure pleasure rippling through her. He alternated his touches, making her frenzied. Faster and harder, then slow and soft, then fast once again. She was so desperate for him that he had scarcely pleasured her for any time when she came on a cry, thrusting herself shamelessly into his hand, grinding down on his straining cock as she did so.

He caught her nipple between his teeth and gently nipped, still working her, draining every last bit of pleasure from her and then demanding more. When his middle finger slid inside her to the knuckle, she moaned, arching her back and rolling her hips to bring him deeper.

It was good, but not good enough.

"I want your cock," she told him, nearly mindless. "I want you inside me."

He made a strangled sound, and then he was furiously unbuttoning the fall of his trousers. His cock sprang free. She rode it, his hot hardness sliding along her cunny in the promise of more.

He angled himself to her entrance, and then he released her nipple. "Come up onto your knees."

She obeyed his instruction, rising over him on the smooth squab. One of his hands settled on her waist. "Now sit on me. Take my cock."

Tentatively, she lowered herself on him. As before, she was unprepared for the initial stretch, the unusual invasion of him, thick and long and hard. But then he guided her down all the way, and he was buried deep, and there had never been a more glorious sensation in the world.

She was sure of it.

"You are in me," she said with wonder, rather amazed the act could be accomplished this way.

She had never supposed it could.

"Yes." He tugged her lips to his, kissing her fiercely, passionately, before breaking away. "Now ride me, my love. Take your pleasure from me."

With his help, she did, rising on her knees until he almost slid from her wetness before sinking down on him. Again and again, until the rhythm and the sheer pleasure carried her away. She was no longer a separate being. Instead, they were one, joined together in body, heart, and soul.

He suckled her breasts as she rode him, aware of everything—the carriage moving over the road, the flick of his tongue over her nipples, the stroke of his cock deep, so deep. The bliss was there, within her reach. His thumb stroked over her clitoris.

"Yes, love," he crooned. "Come on my cock. Make me spend inside you."

She rocked on him, allowing him to help her find an even more pleasurable angle and pace. His sinful words and mouth proved too much. She came apart on a violent burst that stole her breath from her lungs and had her tipping back her head in a silent cry of sheer ecstasy. Holding her tight, he pushed inside her, until he too was spending, his seed filling her with warmth.

For a moment, she could do nothing but slump against him in a sated delirium, heart threatening to race from her breast, her ears ringing from the force of her release. Gradually, lucidity returned in the form of his palm stroking up and down her spine, his whispered words of love in her ear, his lips on her cheek.

Neither of them spoke for a time, the only sounds in the carriage the jangling of tack, the plodding of hooves, and the other street sounds beyond. At last, Pen moved, lifting her head from Garrick's shoulder to take in the sight of the man she loved.

Her husband.

"Surely that was only one tour of Mayfair," she said, feeling impish.

Garrick threw back his head and laughed, the sound making joy swell within her. "And that is one of many reasons why I made you mine, Lady Lordly."

Pen covered Lord Lordly's smiling lips with hers.

THANK you for reading Pen and Garrick's story! I hope it made you laugh and swoon in equal measure and that, like me, you adore a haughty hero who falls hard for his lady.

Do read on for a bonus excerpt from *Sutton's Seduction*,

Book Four in *The Sinful Suttons* series, featuring the sinfully handsome Hart Sutton, who is determined to find answers about his missing brother, Logan. He just may fall for the daughter of the man he suspects responsible along the way…

Please consider leaving an honest review of *Sutton's Surrender.* Reviews are greatly appreciated! If you'd like to keep up to date with my latest releases and series news, sign up for my newsletter here or follow me on Amazon or BookBub. Join my reader's group on Facebook for bonus content, early excerpts, giveaways, and more.

~

Sutton's Seduction
The Sinful Suttons
Book Four

Lady Emma Morgan is desperate. After her father's gambling debts leave her family in penury, she settles upon the only solution to preserving her younger sister's chance for future happiness. Already deemed unmarriageable from a scandal in her first season, Emma will sell herself to the highest bidder.

Hart Sutton is a merciless rogue who trades in the darkest secrets of polite London society. When he learns of a possible connection between the Earl of Haldringham and his missing brother, Hart puts a plan into motion to ruin the man. He buys the earl's eldest daughter's innocence on the auction block with every intention of destroying her, too.

He never supposed Lady Emma would stir him in a way no woman has before or that he would be thoroughly smitten by her intelligence and loyalty. Much to her surprise, Emma is developing feelings for the gruff, fierce man who takes her under his wing. But with each passing day, the looming truth threatens both their happiness and their carefully shielded hearts.

Chapter One

London, 1816

He had just lost more blunt in one week with an earl's daughter than he had ever spent in his bleeding life. But the need for revenge was a damned cruel mistress, and Hart Sutton was determined to seize vengeance using every means at his disposal. Including the masked woman who had joined him in the Rose Room at The Garden of Flora. A woman who ought to have been gliding through a ballroom at Rivendale's on the other side of London, holding court as she sipped lemonade and waved her fan.

Instead, Lady Emma Morgan was scantily dressed, her bare feet pale and absurdly elegant, devoid of stockings. Madame Laurent, the bawd who owned and operated the exclusive house of ill repute in which they stood, had dressed Lady Emma in a revealing gown reminiscent of a Grecian goddess. The pale mounds of her breasts were on display, a slit in her gown opening to reveal the luscious curve of her calf and thigh. Her golden curls were unbound, streaming down her back.

He had no doubt that every man in the room where her virginity had just been auctioned off had desired her. But Hart alone would have her. Not because he wanted her or because he was beset by some perverse desire to despoil an innocent.

Rather, it was because of who she was and what she represented.

Lady Emma Morgan would bring him one step closer to finding his missing brother, Logan. Or at least aid Hart in discovering what had happened to him.

"You are staring, sir," she observed, her dulcet voice soft and hesitant.

For some reason, he had imagined she would speak coldly, with the crisp accent of an aristocrat born to look down her nose at the world around her.

"Can a man not admire that for which he has paid?" he asked curtly, reminding himself that, whatever happened between himself and Lady Emma, he was not meant to find any bit of this business pleasant. "And so dearly, too. Quite a price for one week of a woman's commodity."

He was being crude, but he could not afford to show her kindness.

She stiffened, her lashes lowering to veil her thoughts. Although the silk mask she had worn on the dais to guard her features remained to shield her face from him, beneath it, her full, pink lips thinned. No one was meant to know she was the eldest daughter of the Earl of Haldringham. And no one did except Hart and Madame Laurent. Lady Emma's wicked secret remained safe.

For now.

"Of course you may look your fill," she said then, her lower lip trembling ever so slightly.

Why did he feel as if he had just kicked a puppy?

She held herself so stiffly, immobile, as if she were fashioned of porcelain rather than flesh. Telling himself he would show her no mercy, he clasped his hands behind his back and paced in a slow circle around her. It was his intention to unnerve her. To harden his conscience against what must be done.

He had a moment to admire the glossy fall of hair down her back and the flare of her hips, lovingly outlined by her gown, before she cast him a curious glance over her shoulder.

"Have you done this before?" she asked.

There was a bit of boldness in her, then. Some bravado. Interesting. But he was the one in control here, not her.

He continued his perambulation, stopping before her once more, and decided to ignore her query. "What I do is none of your business. Remove your mask."

"I..." Her words trailed off, and her tongue flicked out to wet her lips. "Madame Laurent assured me I would be entitled to remain anonymous."

He closed the polite space between them, trying not to notice the scent of jasmine teasing his senses. "You were to remain anonymous for the auction, my dear. Not to the man who owns you, body and soul, for the next sennight."

The sharp hiss of her intake of breath was his sole gratification. Otherwise, Lady Emma remained stoic and proud.

"You do not own me," she denied at last. "I fear you have mistaken the manner of auction this was."

"No." He flashed her a grim grin. "I haven't, my dear. But fret not. I very much look forward to spending the next week proving otherwise."

Want more? Get *Sutton's Seduction* now!

AUTHOR'S NOTE

As always, the cant speech used by the Suttons has been sourced mostly from *The Memoirs of James Hardy Vaux* (1819) and Grose's *Dictionary of the Vulgar Tongue* (1811). Rivendale's is a product of my imagination, as are the other establishments mentioned in this book, aside from Almack's. (You may recognize Mr. Duncan Kirkwood and The Duke's Bastard from my Sins and Scoundrels series. You can find his happily ever after in *Prince of Persuasion*.)

DON'T MISS SCARLETT'S OTHER ROMANCES!

Complete Book List

HISTORICAL ROMANCE

Heart's Temptation

A Mad Passion (Book One)

Rebel Love (Book Two)

Reckless Need (Book Three)

Sweet Scandal (Book Four)

Restless Rake (Book Five)

Darling Duke (Book Six)

The Night Before Scandal (Book Seven)

Wicked Husbands

Her Errant Earl (Book One)

Her Lovestruck Lord (Book Two)

Her Reformed Rake (Book Three)

Her Deceptive Duke (Book Four)

Her Missing Marquess (Book Five)

Her Virtuous Viscount (Book Six)

League of Dukes
Nobody's Duke (Book One)
Heartless Duke (Book Two)
Dangerous Duke (Book Three)
Shameless Duke (Book Four)
Scandalous Duke (Book Five)
Fearless Duke (Book Six)

Notorious Ladies of London
Lady Ruthless (Book One)
Lady Wallflower (Book Two)
Lady Reckless (Book Three)
Lady Wicked (Book Four)
Lady Lawless (Book Five)
Lady Brazen (Book 6)

Unexpected Lords
The Detective Duke (Book One)
The Playboy Peer (Book Two)

The Wicked Winters
Wicked in Winter (Book One)
Wedded in Winter (Book Two)
Wanton in Winter (Book Three)
Wishes in Winter (Book 3.5)
Willful in Winter (Book Four)
Wagered in Winter (Book Five)
Wild in Winter (Book Six)
Wooed in Winter (Book Seven)
Winter's Wallflower (Book Eight)
Winter's Woman (Book Nine)
Winter's Whispers (Book Ten)
Winter's Waltz (Book Eleven)

Winter's Widow (Book Twelve)
Winter's Warrior (Book Thirteen)

The Sinful Suttons
Sutton's Spinster (Book One)
Sutton's Sins (Book Two)
Sutton's Surrender (Book Three)
Sutton's Seduction (Book Four)

Sins and Scoundrels
Duke of Depravity
Prince of Persuasion
Marquess of Mayhem
Sarah
Earl of Every Sin
Duke of Debauchery

Second Chance Manor
The Matchmaker and the Marquess by Scarlett Scott
The Angel and the Aristocrat *by Merry Farmer*
The Scholar and the Scot *by Caroline Lee*
The Venus and the Viscount by Scarlett Scott
The Buccaneer and the Bastard *by Merry Farmer*
The Doxy and the Duke *by Caroline Lee*

Stand-alone Novella
Lord of Pirates

CONTEMPORARY ROMANCE
Love's Second Chance
Reprieve (Book One)
Perfect Persuasion (Book Two)
Win My Love (Book Three)

DON'T MISS SCARLETT'S OTHER ROMANCES!

Coastal Heat

Loved Up (Book One)

ABOUT THE AUTHOR

USA Today and Amazon bestselling author Scarlett Scott writes steamy Victorian and Regency romance with strong, intelligent heroines and sexy alpha heroes. She lives in Pennsylvania and Maryland with her Canadian husband, adorable identical twins, and two dogs.

A self-professed literary junkie and nerd, she loves reading anything, but especially romance novels, poetry, and Middle English verse. Catch up with her on her website http://www.scarlettscottauthor.com/. Hearing from readers never fails to make her day.

Scarlett's complete book list and information about upcoming releases can be found at http://www.scarlettscottauthor.com/.

Connect with Scarlett! You can find her here:

Join Scarlett Scott's reader group on Facebook for early excerpts, giveaways, and a whole lot of fun!

Sign up for her newsletter here

https://www.tiktok.com/@authorscarlettscott

facebook.com/AuthorScarlettScott
twitter.com/scarscoromance
instagram.com/scarlettscottauthor
bookbub.com/authors/scarlett-scott
amazon.com/Scarlett-Scott/e/B004NW8N2I
pinterest.com/scarlettscott

Made in the USA
Columbia, SC
03 October 2023

23836511R00138